SPACE CADETS

ROBIN PAWLAK

Robin Pawlak 09/18

MOUNTVIEW

Space Cadets
Copyright © 2018 by Robin Pawlak

Edited by Micah Scotti Kole and
Dawn Christine Jonckowski.

Cover art © 2018 by Zoe Foster

Visit the author's website at robinpawlak.com

Mountview Publishing

ISBN 978-1-7752199-0-3

If you're going to write a book,
you should probably have someone around
who is foolish enough to actually believe you can do it,
and wise enough to recognize when you need to be reminded of that fact.

I married that person over thirty years ago.

This is for her.

The world of reality has its limits; the world of imagination is boundless.

—Jean-Jacques Rousseau

1   House Arrest

Casey floored the gas pedal and the silver Lamborghini whined like a jet, acceleration thrusting us back into the grey leather seats. The sports car sliced through the almost deserted district on the edge of downtown, ramshackle warehouses and abandoned stores on either side of the street zipping past our windows in a blur. The road ahead lay empty, apart from a few pieces of litter that had been caught by a puff of wind.

The speedometer hit one sixty. Red and blue lights flashing in the side mirror showed the police cruiser, still less than a block behind us—two 12-year-olds on the run, accused of a crime we didn't commit.

"Faster!" I shouted above the blaring siren.

"This *is* faster!" Casey's cool blue eyes focused on the road ahead.

We faced a dead end several blocks down the street. *Shoot.* On a straightaway, there was no way the cop car would be able to catch us, but here we'd need to be creative. I searched for somewhere—an alley, a side road—where we could lose them.

My twin sister slammed on the brakes as a white delivery truck lurched out of an alley to our left. I braced for a crash, but Casey had other plans. "Woohoo!" she cried, as her foot jumped over to the gas pedal and she cranked the steering wheel hard.

We skidded right, the sound of squealing tires filling our ears. Shooting past the truck, we missed its front bumper by a hair, but now had another problem. "Casey!" I shouted as we barreled straight toward a vacant store.

"I see it." She yanked the steering wheel back to the left, but too late. "Hold on!"

The front tires hit the curb, hurling us both forward against our seat belts; then we were airborne. The sports car soared over the sidewalk and smashed through the store window, sending a shower of glass in all directions. For one bizarre moment, we seemed to be gliding through the air in ultra-slow motion. I remember two things. First, a lone mannequin that stood guard in the forsaken shop, and how the Lamborghini's gracefully sloping hood clipped off her bald head as the car descended, flipping it back onto the windshield with a crack, and then off out of sight. You don't see that every day. And the second thing: screaming. Mine, and Casey's.

We landed with a jolt that snapped our chins to our chests. The sports car plowed through an assortment of shelving and boxes with a din of clanging and crashing, in spite of Casey hauling on the steering wheel and jamming the brakes. We were tossed about like rag dolls as the car slid along the brick wall on the far side of the shop, halting with a bone-rattling thump when it hit the back wall. The Lamborghini's engine snarled one last time, then fell silent.

I shook my head and took a breath to collect my wits. Was that blood on my jeans? No. Jam from breakfast. I seemed to be all right. A loose brick dropped from the wall onto the fender.

I turned to my sister. "Are you okay?"

She scowled. "Yeah, yeah. Let's get outta here!" She took one look at her door, pressed firmly against the wall, and said, "Go! Your side!"

I pulled the handle, elbowed the door open and burst out into the great cloud of dust that we had kicked up. I blinked and rubbed my eyes with the sleeve of my black and white striped rugby shirt. Casey scrambled out after me, coughing.

Quiet. No siren. Where were they? Beyond the big open space where the store window had been, we could see the

3

truck stopped in the middle of the road, driver's door open. But no one in sight.

Casey and I exchanged glances, and she nodded toward the road. We edged forward, Casey in the lead, heading for the right side of the window. Near the opening, I noticed the mannequin head and bent down to pick it up.

"Simon!" Casey hissed. She peeked out through the front of the store and beckoned me to join her. When she saw what I was doing, she shook her head. "Hurry up!"

"What is it?"

"The cop car. Look!"

Peering around Casey, I followed a trail of skid marks that led to the police cruiser, its front end crumpled against the side of an overfull garbage dumpster. The bin had once contained even more trash, but much of its slimy, stinking contents had spewed out onto the previously shiny vehicle. The truck driver, helping the officers out of their car, spotted us and pointed in our direction.

"Let's go!" Casey jumped out onto the street, darted off to the left, and cut down a narrow alley beside the store. I raced after her, turned the corner, then paused. The old brick warehouse beside the store cast a shadow over the garbage-strewn lane, and I couldn't help but wonder what dangers might lie hidden in its darker corners.

Back in the street, one of the officers barked into his radio, "Unit 511 requesting backup at Maple and Kole."

Casey, nearing the end of the alley, called back to me, "Simon! Hurry up!" Her impatient-bordering-on-angry voice.

4

She was right. This was no time to hesitate. I sprinted ahead into the shadows.

Our pursuer continued his message. "We are on foot in pursuit of two suspects—juveniles; one male, one female, both Caucasian. Female is tall, average build, medium length blond hair. Male: slim, short light brown hair; also tall—"

"What!" Casey had stopped running.

"What is it?" *Had she run into trouble?*

"You're not tall!" she said.

"Casey! What are you . . . ?" I caught up to her, and found her awaiting me with arms folded across the front of her purple T-shirt. The cops had entered the alley. They would be on us in seconds. "Let's go! They're gaining on us!" I turned to go, then stopped. "And what do you mean I'm not tall?"

"*I'm* tall. You're short."

"Last time Dad measured us, you were barely a centimetre taller!" *Why did she always have to argue?*

"Okay." She shrugged. "I'm not tall; just above average. And *you* are short."

"I'm *not* short! I'm as tall as most kids."

"Not as tall as me."

It was always a competition with her. It didn't matter what. Taller, smarter. Better. I should have just ignored her, but why should she get her way all the time? "Not as *bossy* as you either!"

"Bossy? Bossy!" Casey's eyes narrowed. "I'm *not* bossy! And I *told* you to stop saying that!"

Obviously angry, she'd probably get us into even more trouble if I didn't stop. "Okay! Fine. I'm short, and you're . . . super nice. Let's go! They'll catch us!" I started to run, but she didn't follow. "Casey . . ."

"Oh, you don't wanna get caught? No problem." She pulled out her gun, which had been tucked in the waist of her jeans.

"Casey, what—"

"BAM!"

"Are you nuts?" I shrieked. "You shot me!"

"It's an empty water pistol, Simon. You'll live."

"You always wreck the game!"

"What do you mean?" She smiled sweetly. "I did it just for you. Killing you will keep it . . . *short.*" She stepped forward and gave me a little pat on the head.

I guess that's when I jumped on her. I can't remember all the details; it happened so fast and ended so quickly.

Mom put a stop to it. "Hey! What on earth do you two think you're doing?"

Bashing each other with our fists seemed like the obvious answer, but probably not the one she wanted. Adults are funny that way. So we said nothing, and Mom stood there waiting with several bags of groceries hanging from each hand.

"Don't look at me," Casey said. "He started it!"

"Are you kidding me? You did!"

She looked at Mom and shrugged.

"She shot me!" I paused, realizing that I might need to explain this a little. "Well, not *really*. I mean, she doesn't *actually* have a gun, but . . ."

Mom sighed. Deeply. "How many times have I told you that if you're going to run around, it's either downstairs or outside? Now here I am breaking up a fistfight in the middle of our living room, and our guests will be here any minute!" She shook her head, turned and marched into the kitchen with her load, calling back to us, "Casey, empty the dishwasher. And Simon, I already told you to take the garbage out!"

With Mom so busy getting ready, we escaped with only the tongue-lashing and a couple of minor chores. Maybe she figured that the upcoming visit would be punishment enough. See, the company was Aunt Emily, Uncle Robert and Cousin Ernest. And Cousin Ernest—well . . .

My mother used the word *obnoxious* to describe him once when she thought my sister and I weren't listening. Casey insists *snotty* suits him better. Anyway, we're not allowed to call him either one, so we go with *Cousin* Ernest. I suppose the *Cousin* part reminds us that we have to put up with him because we're related. It's probably also the reason none of us have killed him yet.

Considering what he was about to do, that might have been our best bet. A pre-emptive strike. But then I guess none of this would have happened.

2   Cousin Ernest

Cousin Ernest leaned over and whispered in his mother's ear.

"No, pumpkin," she said. "We discussed this earlier, remember?"

"But, Mommy . . ." I always thought that if weasels could talk, they'd sound like Cousin Ernest.

"After lunch, my little prince. Then there will be no distractions, and you will have everyone's full attention." She patted him lovingly on his chubby little cheeks. It was hard to believe this kid was 13 years old.

He'd already tried a couple times since we'd all sat down for lunch, but he didn't get his way, which was weird. I was getting curious. What was so important that we all had to wait until just the right moment, even if it meant saying *no* to His Royal Pumpkiness?

I was the last to finish dessert. The second I set down my spoon, Cousin Ernest sprang to his feet. "*Now* can I get it?"

This time, Aunt Emily said *yes*. Cousin Ernest shot out the door.

"He has been so upset because he hasn't had a chance to show you last year's report card yet," she explained. "I forgot it at home when we visited last time. I've been hearing about it ever since!" She shook her head, but her smile said that she thought he was just the cutest thing.

I looked at Casey. "Garbage," I whispered.

"Tell me about it."

"No," I hissed. "The garbage. I forgot."

It took a second. Then she got it. She turned to Mom. "Simon didn't take the garbage out!"

I jumped up. "Sorry. I'll do it right now!"

"I better go with him." She pushed her chair back. "To make sure he does it."

We were out the door before anyone could say a word.

*   *   *

After taking out the trash, we went downstairs. Casey had wanted to play video games, but I convinced her that a board game was a better plan. Cousin Ernest loves video games. This way, he'd have the console to himself and, hopefully, leave us alone.

But no. Because when he joined us in the family room, it wasn't to play games.

"Hey guys, look at my report card!" He waved a piece of paper above his head like a flag in a parade.

Casey didn't even look up. Bent over the game, her blonde bangs made a little curtain that blocked out everything in the room except for the game board. "Uh . . . we're in the middle of *Frontier* right now." She rolled the dice. "Maybe later."

Sitting up made me an easier target. Cousin Ernest settled in beside me and held out the sheet so I could get a really good look. Then he paused for a whole second before announcing, "Straight A's. The Physical Education mark doesn't count, of course." It was a C-. "Everyone knows it isn't a real subject," he explained. "Besides, the teacher is completely unfair. He took off marks because I 'don't participate'. I tried to explain that I tire easily, but he wouldn't listen."

Casey raised herself up just long enough for a quick eye-roll in my direction. Our cousin didn't notice.

"My English teacher says I have an exceptional vocabulary." He placed a thick finger on the English Language Arts grade. "I'm sure that's part of the reason for the A, although my grammar is also excellent."

Great. He'd launched into a subject-by-subject breakdown.

"I've noticed that many of my peers simply don't seem to care about the fundamentals of the English language." His eyes were half closed, his chin slightly raised. "To be honest, I'm deeply concerned about our generation."

I couldn't take it any more. Time for plan B. Our dear cousin kept blathering away, but I interrupted him. "Hey, guys! Let's play hide-and-seek!"

Casey looked up, head tilted, one eyebrow raised.

Cousin Ernest crinkled his stubby nose. "But—"

"Come on!" I grinned like a cheesy TV salesman. "It'll be fun!" Then I caught my sister's eye with a sideways glance. "We'll hide first."

She got the message. Her tiny smile widened. The next second she grabbed my arm and dragged me to the door.

"Count to 200!" I called back to our cousin, who we left bewildered and alone.

Casey ran off into the guest room, but I paused at the door across the hall from it. Dad had put up a sign on the door of his workroom: *DANGER! KEEP OUT.*

Our father is an inventor. I mean, he has a regular job, like most dads. But his hobby is what he really loves, and he spends most of his free time in his little room.

Once when we were about five, he took Casey and me in to show us his stuff. She reached for something she shouldn't have, and I tried to stop her. We scuffled, and one

11

of Dad's contraptions ended up in pieces on the floor. Since then, Dad's room has been out of bounds.

But the sign was new. He'd been in there an awful lot lately. Weird . . .

I turned and went into the spare room to find Casey wriggling out from under the bed. "Too easy," she said. "He'll find us right away." Then she darted past me into the hall.

By the time I got out there, I found Dad's door open. She stood in the middle of the room with her back to me, about three steps in. The only light came from the open door. "Casey!" I said, trying to keep my voice down so Cousin Ernest wouldn't hear. "Are you nuts?"

She turned to face me. "What?"

"We can't hide in here!"

"Sure we can."

"What if Dad finds out?"

She shrugged. "He won't."

"Didn't you see the sign on the door?"

"Huh?" She stepped forward to check it out. "Whoa. Awesome!" She raised her eyebrows, grinned, then turned to go back into the room.

"What! Casey, it says 'Danger!'"

"Simon, seriously." She turned around and opened her arms, palms upturned. "What could happen?"

I opened my mouth to reply, but she interrupted me.

"Look, do you want Cousin Ernest to find us?"

"No, but—"

"Good." She scanned the room in search of a hiding spot. "Cuz this'll be the last place he looks!"

I glanced back toward the family room.

I could hear Cousin Ernest counting. ". . . 76, 77 . . ."

Casey called to me from deeper in Dad's room. "Hey, turn on the light."

"No. C'mon, let's hide in the laundry room. There's—"

"Forget it. First place he'll look."

"Fine. Then we'll just—"

"Would you stop being such a little chicken?"

I hated it when she called me that. And I hated that it felt like sometimes it might be a little bit true. But I couldn't shake the feeling that this was a bad idea.

Back down the hall I heard Cousin Ernest again. ". . . 128, 129—"

One twenty-nine? What! No way he could be that far already. *Little cheater!*

"Simon!" Casey hissed.

That's it! I decided. *I'm going in.*

Since then I've chosen to blame my sister and cousin for what happened next.

3   Ready or Not . . .

Casey was fumbling around off in the corner. "Hey. What's this?"

I flicked on the light and closed the door. Turning around, I couldn't believe what I saw. "The rocket!"

When we were little, we used to play 'space' in the laundry room. Our rocket was a very old shower stall, with three white metal walls and a plastic shower curtain hung across the opening. It used to be in the downstairs bathroom, but Dad replaced it with a newer one.

The memories flooded back. We decorated the inside with markers, tape and pieces of cardboard to make control panels, gauges and view screens. The showerhead was attached with a hose, and it became the microphone we used to communicate with Mission Control. We flew missions to every corner of the galaxy. I smiled. "Casey, remember the time we—"

"Hey, look at this." The rocket now had a metal door that wasn't there when we were younger. Casey had already jerked it open and was halfway inside. "Whoa!"

Inside the rocket, real buttons and gauges had replaced our old cardboard ones, and the microphone wasn't attached to a hose any more, but a cable.

"Um . . ." I wanted a closer look, but this wasn't just an old shower stall anymore. I remembered the sign. *DANGER!*

". . . two hundred!" *Cousin Ernest!* "Ready or not, here I co-o-me!"

"Quick!" Casey dropped down on the big old wooden chair that served as our pilot's seat. "Turn off the light!"

I rushed to the light switch, then fumbled back through the darkness. I felt first for the rocket, then the opening. Casey's hand met mine, and she pulled me in.

"Here," she said. "Sit down."

It was harder than it sounded. The rocket was small, and we weren't little anymore. She squished over, and in spite of some awkward bumbling, we managed to squeeze ourselves onto the chair.

A door squeaked open on the other side of the hall. *Good.* Cousin Cheaterface was close, but heading in the wrong direction.

"Close the door," Casey whispered.

"Um . . ." I began. I still wasn't comfortable with this. "He's in the spare bedroom. Let's make a run for it. We can—"

She sighed, reached past me, and after fumbling for a moment, found the handle. She yanked the door, and it whacked my elbow.

"Ow!"

"Well, get outta the way!" She grabbed my arm with her other hand, and then pulled the door closed with a loud thump.

"Nice one!" I rubbed my aching elbow.

"Shhh!"

I hated it when she shushed me. Who did she think she was, my mother? I'd had enough. I didn't care anymore whether Ernest found us or not. I reached for the door and gave it a push. It didn't budge.

"Hey!" Casey growled. "What're you doing?"

"The door's locked!"

"Don't open the—" Pause. "Whatta ya mean, locked?"

She reached across for the door again. This time she leaned into me on the way by, so I shoved her arm away. Her elbow jerked up and caught me under the chin, knocking my head against the back of the rocket. I grunted, shook my head, and—

The workroom door opened.

We froze. Footsteps. Right to the shower stall. "Aha!" crowed a snotty voice on the other side of the door. "Found you!" The rocket rattled as he tried to open the door. "You have to come out now."

"We can't," I told him. "It's locked."

"Unlock it," whined Cousin Sherlock.

"We can't," repeated Casey. "Turn on the light and we'll look for a latch."

"I already did."

It was still totally dark inside the rocket. Dad must have put a roof on it.

Casey took charge. "Simon, feel around on the door." Then she called out to our cousin. "Ernest, look for some way to open it from your side."

He tried the handle again. The whole stall shook, leaving me feeling like a bean in a maraca, but the door stayed closed.

"Isn't there a key," Casey said, "or a special latch or something?"

He was quiet for a moment. "Well, I'm not sure what they do, but . . . there are some buttons here . . ."

"No!" I cried. *DANGER!* "No buttons!"

But it was too late.

A whirring sound arose, like a jet preparing for takeoff. The underside of the showerhead glowed an eerie yellow-green. Casey jumped to her feet and grabbed it off the wall. "What the . . ." It shone even brighter now, its light filling the rocket. The gauges had sprung to life, and several red lights flashed angrily at us, accompanied by urgent beeping.

"Shut it off!" I hollered.

"I don't know how!" Cousin Ernest howled.

And that was the last thing I heard, because at that instant, a blinding light streaked from the showerhead through my eyeballs and bounced off the inside of the back of my skull.

4　Waking Up

I opened my eyes. Blinked.

Problem: I couldn't see anything.

For a moment, I thought that maybe I was dead, but the throbbing in my head told me I was probably still alive. I'd had headaches before, but this one seemed to be about two sizes bigger than my head and trying to bust out through my skull to find a better home.

Then I remembered that it had been completely dark inside the cubicle, which was a relief. I wasn't blind.

Something hit my face. A hand, I figured. Casey's, most likely. I decided that I was upset about this, so I told her just how I felt about it. "Zurble," I said.

I had planned to say something more like, "Dear sister, please do not strike me." Or, if I'm being honest, "Stop! Idiot!" But it didn't matter, because all that came out was, "Zurble."

Casey seemed to be having problems too, because she replied with, "Awawwa babba."

I was a little confused. "Bum bum?" I asked. Well, at least I was starting to use real words.

Our minds began to clear a little, and after relearning how to use our brains, tongues and lips, we started to make some sense. Still, it took a good 15 minutes before we were even able to understand our situation. Apparently we were locked inside some kind of homemade brain-baking machine that seemed to have turned us into morons. And since Cousin Ernest was obviously long gone, we were on our own.

In the end, we only got out by accident. In an attempt to regain control of my limbs, my flailing arm flipped up into the air and flopped down on something. Which went *ka-chunk* and opened the door—which I fell out of, followed by Casey. Who landed on top of me.

"So," Casey said. "There was . . . a latch."

"Yuphh," I replied. I was having trouble speaking again, although now it had nothing to do with having had my brains toasted. This time it was because there was a sister on my head.

We eventually sorted ourselves out and rejoined everyone upstairs. I was relieved, thinking we'd managed to solve our problem and leave the whole mess behind us.

I was wrong.

5 Space, Please

The TV remote soared across the living room, struck the edge of the entertainment unit, and clattered to the hardwood in pieces.

"No way!" Casey stood on her feet, yelling at the television.

"Yes," said a cheesy game show host, almost as if he had heard her, "it's true. If you have boanthropy, you believe you are a cow."

Casey slumped back into the armchair. "Stupid."

I stared at the shattered remote. Good thing no one else was around. About the time we made it out of the rocket,

Cousin Ernest had told his mother he wasn't feeling well, and they'd left soon after. Our parents went out to run some errands, and we'd plopped ourselves in front of the TV. The effects of our little accident had started to wear off, but we were still pretty out of it.

I turned to my sister. "Great. You better be able to fix—"

Her death glare stopped me cold. I thought about dealing with it myself, but I didn't want to get off the couch. Casey would have some explaining to do when Mom and Dad got home, but that was her problem.

"Next question!" said Gameshow Man, like this was the most exciting news ever. "For 200 points: Which country has the most cows?"

A plump woman in a flowery dress buzzed in. "America?"

Casey sat up. "No! India."

"Sorry, Melinda," replied Mr. Gameshow, who didn't look sorry. "The correct answer is *India*, with well over 300 million!"

"Yes!" Casey fist-pumped and leaned forward, ready to tackle the next question. The game show had perked her up.

"Now for the final question in the *Cows* category!" Big, cheesy smile.

Wow, I thought. *Cows.* I'm not a huge fan of game shows. But when we first sat down, Casey had the remote (of course), and this was where she'd taken us.

"For 500 points!" He paused to allow the studio audience to applaud wildly. "Which state is home to the World Championship Cow Chip Throwing Contest?"

There's a championship for tossing cow turds?

"Oh!" Casey grabbed hold of her knees. "Ohio! No . . . no, that's the duct tape festival."

"Seriously?" I asked.

She didn't hear me. "Nebraska?" She shook her head. "Wait . . . Nebraska, or Kansas?" She glanced at me. "Simon? Which one?"

"Sorry, you're out of time," the host said, like a doctor delivering bad news. "The correct answer is . . . Oklahoma!"

"Aaaaaaaaaaaahh!" Casey leapt to her feet and slapped her hands onto her head. "I should've gotten that one!"

Apparently, mood swings were a symptom of being zapped by a showerhead. I took the lamp off the end table between us and moved it onto the couch beside me, out of her reach. Just in case she felt the need to throw something again.

"Bertram, you're in the lead." The host straightened his tie. "Choose a category."

A tall, bearded contestant in a tweed jacket replied, "*Space* please, Tom."

Space. Now there was a topic! *Space Journey* was my favourite TV series. I'd watched every single episode at least once—the season finale eight times, and counting. Maybe this game show would be interesting after all.

"Excellent choice!" said Tom. The question popped up on the screen as he read it aloud. "Bertram, for 100 points: Which two elements are most commonly found beneath the surface of the planet Saturn?"

Well, so much for interesting. To think that Casey had flipped right through a rerun of *Space Journey* before settling on this ridiculous game show. It was the episode that showed my hero, Captain Clark, as a young cadet during a training mission at Zargon base.

Everything around me faded into the background as I imagined myself piloting a small cargo shuttle. I reached for the joystick between my knees and eased it to the right, while my other hand flipped various toggle switches on the console between the two seats.

The spacecraft banked gracefully to starboard as it continued its ascent from the surface of Zargon. The window to my right showed the dry grey-brown soil of the almost-deserted moon. As the little ship looped around, I glimpsed a few of the buildings on the outer edge of the base. The grey and white structures made it look like a drab little model town.

The computer beeped, and its female voice said, "Altitude: 500 metres."

"Roger that." It was time to prepare for the jump to lightspeed.

I straightened the vessel out, then tapped the touchscreen controls. The monitor above showed the flight plan that had been preprogrammed into the computer.

Another beep. "Altitude: 1,000 metres. Please prepare for transition to autopilot."

I pressed the button labeled *ANS* for Automated Navigation System. The joystick went limp in my hand, then retracted underneath the control panel. The craft shifted slightly.

Another beep. "Autopilot engaged." The computer voice was pleasant—calm and helpful, but not quite friendly. "Please enter initial speed manually."

My hand jumped to the speed control on the centre console, and my heart thumped with anticipation. *Lightspeed. Oh yeah!* I gripped the handle. Took a breath. Then slid the control forward from *Surge* to *Lightspeed 1*.

A large blue indicator light on the panel in front of me glowed, its brightness gradually increasing, along with the hum of the engines behind me. But still no change in speed. The hum became a roar. Now sound and blue light filled the cargo shuttle's cabin as it shook with the engines' powerful vibrations. *Uh oh.* I leaned forward to scan the gauges and warning lights, wondering if I'd messed up.

My head snapped back and bounced off the headrest. Through the front window, stars smeared into long white streaks that trailed off out of sight as we hurtled through space. The indicator light dimmed, and the engines fell almost silent.

"Lightspeed achieved," droned the computer. "Level 1."

I shook my head, then leaned back in my chair and smiled. *Just like Captain Clark.* Although, I had to admit it had been a lot tougher than it looked on TV.

That probably should have been my clue that something was wrong. I'd always had an amazing imagination. I came up with great ideas, and when I got the chance to drift off into a good daydream it could seem pretty realistic. But this time was different.

I was about to find out exactly how different.

6   ODD

"Control to Commander Andrews. Come in, Commander Andrews." I jumped as the gruff voice barked at me from the near-silence of the ship's cabin.

"Uh . . . yes?" Not very professional.

The message repeated. I scrambled to find a microphone so they could hear me. A rocker switch on the console flashed green, so I jabbed it with my finger. "Commander Andrews here," I said, attempting my deepest, most impressive voice, which cracked.

"Commander, you will be leaving the Casimonian System in approximately sixty seconds. This final message is to confirm your mission and flight path." His voice was like someone banging rocks together.

"Right . . ."

"You are to travel to Marek Base on planet Dopsik. Lieutenant McTaggart will have the supplies ready when you arrive. Have you filed your course?"

"Filed my . . . um . . . course?"

"Commander, has your flight plan been transferred to the central database?" This guy was sounding grumpier by the second.

I searched for something that said *Database* among the dozens of switches, buttons and gauges on the controls spread out before me. *Which one?* A light blinked on the panel to my left, so I pushed the button underneath it. A siren blared and half a dozen other lights flashed.

"Commander, we are receiving your distress signal. Preparing to send a squadron to assist. Confirm."

I hit the button again and everything returned to normal. *Phew!*

"Commander. Please respond!"

"Uh . . . false alarm." I sounded like an idiot. "There was a . . . malfunction."

"Do you need to return to base for repairs?"

"Nope." I should have said *yes*.

There was a pause. "Very well, Commander. Have you downloaded your flight plan to our database?"

Downloaded? Oh! The computer! I opened up the flight plan I'd been looking at earlier, finding a red button labelled *Transfer.* I tapped it and a progress bar popped up on the monitor. "Yay!"

"Uh, come again, Commander?"

Shoot. "Yayy...ess. Yes." I cleared my throat. "Yes, transfer complete."

A few seconds passed. "Very well, Commander. Your mission and flight plan are confirmed. You will be leaving the Casimonian System in fifteen seconds. All further communications will be terminated. Good luck, Commander, and remember this is a supply mission only. Do not engage the enemy unless under direct attack. Control out."

"The enemy? Wait! What enemy?"

No response.

"Commander Andrews to Control! Come in, Control!"

Nothing. I flicked the green switch. Off, on.

"Hello?" First this guy says a bunch of stuff that makes no sense, and then he just stops talking.

Wait a minute. I'm just imagining this, right? I slowly reached out and touched the console, feeling the hard plastic, smooth buttons and cool metal toggle switches. Actually *feeling* them. Like they were real. Fear rushed through my veins like ice water.

I blinked, then looked again. Sure enough, that was my hand, touching—*Wait, what?* Gold material covered my arm. I looked down. Gold shirt, black pants and a crest on the left

30

side of my chest; two black stripes encircling my left bicep. I was dressed like Captain Clark!

I jumped to my feet. Standing in the space between my seat and the cabin wall, I scanned my surroundings. Ahead, a window with a view of the stars. Then a bank of controls, two seats, and behind them, a cargo area. Just like a cargo shuttle on *Space Journey*—but not on TV. Right there, in front of me. *This is crazy!*

I needed to think. It couldn't be real. There had to be an explanation. *This is just a really good daydream. I have a great imagination, right?* That was the solution. *I'll just stop.*

I shook my head and closed my eyes. Opened them. Still in a spaceship.

Stuck in a daydream. How does that happen? My heart raced. Squeezing my eyes shut, I tried imagining myself back home in my living room, but when I opened them there I was, still in space. I took a breath. Tried again. Same thing.

Okay, okay . . . This was not okay. *Calm down . . .* I swallowed hard. *Come on. You're in space. What would Captain Clark do?* But I couldn't think. Instead, my mind went blank and my insides tightened into a little ball of fear. "What do I do?" I screamed.

"Please state your request in the form of a specific question or command," the computer replied.

"Um . . . Hi." Maybe it was only a computer, but talking to someone—some*thing*—comforted me. "I need some help."

"Please state your request in the form of a specific question or command."

"Right . . . uh . . . Where am I?"

"You are on board the Casimonian space shuttle *Valiant*, coordinates 5.327 by 1.092, Grid Beta 1."

Naturally, I responded like any highly trained aerospace officer. "Huh?"

"Please state your request in the form of a specific question or command."

I sighed. She—it—wasn't making this any easier. "I . . . I don't understand you."

"Please state your request in the form—"

"Your words! I don't understand your *words*! Tell me what the *words mean*!"

"Would you like to access the Onboard Digital Dictionary?"

"That would be great."

A message box appeared at the bottom of the screen:

Welcome to the ODD.

Yup. Definitely odd.

The computer spoke again. "I will now display my previous statement on the monitor above the message box. You may access the ODD to assist you with any unfamiliar words." Its earlier message popped up:

You are on board the Casimonian space shuttle Valiant, coordinates 5.327 by 1.092, Grid Beta 1.

Please type the unfamiliar word or phrase in the box below.

I started with the first word I didn't understand:

Casimonian

Along came a new message:

Casimonian (kā-si-mō-nē-ən)

From the planet Casimonia.

Casimonia is the second of seven planets orbiting the star Lumar. It is the third largest planet in the system that bears its name and the only one inhabited by human life.

I stared at the screen, trying to make sense of it. Trying to figure out how I got from my couch to a cargo shuttle. It was like someone had taken my brain and given it a shake; my thoughts were the swirling flakes in a snow globe.

You can do this, Simon. Be cool. "So . . . what? Are you saying this ship is from a planet called Casimonia?"

"Affirmative."

"Affirmative!"

"Please state your request—"

"Aaaa! What do you mean, affirmative?"

"Would you like to access the ODD?"

No. I'd like to smash you into little pixels. "I *know* what *affirmative* means! What I want to know is: How can you say that?"

"Data is transferred electronically to the speech synthesis unit, where it is then converted to—"

"Are you kidding me?" I leaned forward and screamed at the monitor. "I'm losing my mind here, and you're explaining computer technology! Is that seriously what you're doing right now?"

"Affirmative."

I threw back my head, closed my eyes and yelled, "Aaaaaaaaaaaaaaaaaaaaahh!" *Not bad, but not quite enough.* "Aaaaaaaaaaaaaaaaaaaaaaaaahhh!"

Better.

The worst of it was that after all of this, I still wasn't any closer to knowing where I was. I went back to the computer's original message.

Talking to myself has always helped me think. "Okay, I'm on a space shuttle from Casimonia." *Simple enough. Except that it's impossible.* "It's called the *Valiant*." *Also simple. But useless.* Then I got to the coordinates, and the snow globe effect kicked in again.

I considered asking the computer to explain, but after imagining how that conversation might go, decided it wasn't worth it. Then I got a better idea. I thought carefully to make sure I worded the question just right. "Where is Earth?"

For a few seconds, the only sound was the soft hum of the engines.

"Unknown."

"Unknown?"

"Affirmative."

"What do you mean, un—" I caught myself. "Um . . . Why don't you know where Earth is?"

Another pause.

"My database has been programmed to include all of the currently identified stars, planets and satellites in the known universe."

Okay. Now we're getting somewhere.

"Among approximately 40 billion, trillion planets listed, there is no entry for *Earth*."

7   Wish upon a Star

No Earth? My mouth dropped open as I struggled to make sense of what I'd just heard. I couldn't believe this was happening. *What a day. First, Cousin Stupidface electrocutes me, then I end up lost in outer space.*

Then it hit me. *We got zapped, went upstairs, then I ended up here.* Maybe this all had something to do with Dad's machine. *But why—*

"Warning." The computer's expressionless voice interrupted my thoughts. "An alien vessel has entered the ship's defense perimeter. A Level 2 Alert Protocol is recommended."

"What?" I choked down panic. I needed a specific question. "What do I do?"

"Implement a Level 2 Alert Protocol."

Big help. "Yeah, yeah. But what *is* a Level 2 Alert Protocol?"

"A Level 2 Alert Protocol is the standard procedure followed when an alien vessel enters a ship's defense perimeter. During times of war, all such ships are to be regarded as potential threats. Appropriate precautions are strongly advised."

I closed my eyes, took a deep breath, then let it out slowly. *Okay Simon, don't panic.*

"Warning. Alien vessel approaching." This computer wasn't making it any easier to stay calm. "Time to intercept: 4 minutes, 11 seconds. Implement Level 2 Alert Protocol immediately."

"I don't know how!" Then before the computer could correct me, I said, "How do I *do* a Level 2 Alert Protocol?"

"Step One: Perform a preliminary scan of the approaching vessel by typing *S-C-A-N-1* into the keypad on your touchscreen controls."

I followed the directions as quickly as I could. The monitor displayed a detailed description of the alien craft:

The approaching vessel is a **Deathfighter 7**.

The Deathfighter 7 is a destroyer-class starship of the Gamnilian Empire.

Weaponry:

- 2 limited-range density cannons
- 20 class 4 directed energy blasters
- 250 Vextron torpedoes

Warning:

The unannounced appearance of a Deathfighter 7 should be seen as hostile. Implement a Level 3 Alert Protocol immediately.

Hand shaking, I reached for the radio switch, flicking it off and on. "Control! This is *Valiant*! Mayday! Mayday!"

No response. I flipped the switch several more times while calling, "Control! We are under attack! Mayday!" Nothing.

I opened my mouth to ask the computer what to do, then stopped myself. I was sick of wrestling with that stupid thing. I needed to find a solution myself.

"Warning. Two minutes, forty-eight seconds to intercept. Immediate implementation of a—"

"Oh, shut up!" *There. That was a pretty specific command.*

The computer fell silent.

The quiet helped me calm down a little. *You can do this, Simon. You got this far.* Then it hit me. When this all started, I'd been imagining that I was flying a spaceship, and it was going pretty well. I couldn't imagine my way out of here, but maybe I could imagine my way *through*.

I closed my eyes and pictured the cockpit of one of the shuttles from *Space Journey* with the fleet's top pilot, Lieutenant Yamada, at the helm. Having watched so many episodes, I could see it all in my mind almost as clearly as if I was sitting in front of the TV.

Now I just had to copy the lieutenant. With a few taps of the touchscreen, I brought up the navigational controls. *Good. Now for the tricky part.* A hard left. I adjusted a few sliders on the computer and typed in some commands—which involved some guessing. I pressed *Enter.*

The little ship shuddered as it swung to port, throwing me across the center console. I scrambled back into position.

Just one last move. I set my right hand on the speed control, and with the other, grabbed ahold of the control panel. I smiled and imagined myself at the helm of the *Starship Venture*, Captain Clark saying, "Hit it, Mr. Andrews!" And I did. All the way to *Lightspeed 4.*

Instant response. The engines roared, the blue light shone, and the craft shot forward like a rock from a slingshot. *I did it!* Then, just as I relaxed, a siren sounded. Several lights blinked, accompanied by a message flashing across the monitor in large orange letters: WARNING!

The shuttle spun wildly like an off-center teacup ride. The force threw me forward, twisted me around, flung me against the far side of the cabin, and flipped me onto my back on the hard rubber floor behind the seats. After a few turns, it slowed down, giving me the chance to take stock of my surroundings from where I lay stunned on the deck.

The lights were out, with the exception of one emergency lamp on the back wall. I blinked, then winced as I propped myself up on one elbow. I took a moment to rub a sore, stiff neck. I managed to sit up, and peered between the seats to find that apart from a handful of blinking lights, the controls had gone dark. Two words flashed in large red letters on the monitor: COMPUTER OFFLINE.

I hoisted myself to my feet, which were just about the only part of my body that didn't hurt. On my way back to the pilot's seat, I found that I was able to move well enough, so no serious injuries. My headache was definitely back, though.

Now what? The spinning had all but stopped. *Fly away? Tried that. Ask the computer? Call Control? Tried those too.* Time was slipping away and I had no clue why nothing I did was working, or even why I was in space to begin with. *I wish Casey was here. She'd think of something.*

I probably should have been terrified. Maybe I was in shock. But I just tucked up my legs, wrapped my arms around my knees and stared blankly ahead into space. Blackness, stars, and silence.

Then I noticed one star, larger than the others, and growing. *Wait . . . That's not a star. It's a ship.*

I watched, helpless and numb, as it drew closer. All I could think of was my sister, my twin. We'd been together—played together, fought together, laughed together—our whole lives. I closed my eyes; it was easy to picture her face, to hear her laugh. What would she think of all this? I imagined her sitting in the seat beside me, staring out the window with her eyes wide, saying—

"What's going on?"

It was just like she was really there.

"Simon! I'm talking to you."

I spun in my seat. My eyes popped open along with my mouth. "What!"

Casey stared right back at me.

"How did *you* get here?"

"I . . ." She turned and gawked at the gigantic starship approaching us. "I have *no* idea."

8   The Gamnilians Say Hello

Casey turned back toward me, looked down at my uniform, then scanned the ship's cabin. "I was . . . watching TV . . ." A frown cut across her pale face, and she shook her head. "Where am I?"

I shrugged. "I've been trying to figure *that* out for a while."

She cocked her head. "How long have you been here?"

"Um . . . I dunno . . . maybe an hour?"

"Whadda you mean?" She threw up her hands. "You were sitting right beside me in the living room!"

I shrugged again. I'd hoped Casey would be able to help; instead she was grilling me. "Yeah, well, I was watching the game show, then . . ."

"Then what? How'd you get here?"

"I don't know. I just . . ." I didn't like talking about my imagination with Casey; I felt stupid. I gestured toward the enormous battleship that had slowed down as it moved into position. "Do you really wanna talk about this right now?"

She looked out at a spacecraft the size of a major shopping mall. "Right." Leaning over to search the control panel in front of me, she asked, "How d'ya turn this thing on?"

"Beats me! It just shut down the last time I—"

Casey poked something that looked just like the power button on our laptop. The computer played three cheerful little notes, and the monitor read *Welcome!*

Oh. That was easy . . .

She glanced at the grey-brown alien ship, then back at the controls. "You have any idea how to fly this thing?"

"Uh . . . sort of."

"Know how to turn on the engines?"

"Um . . ."

She shot me an annoyed glance. "Just get outta my way," she said, motioning for me to switch places with her.

"I'm the pilot!"

"Yeah. Obviously."

"It's not my fault! I was—"

"Aaaah!" An orange streak leapt from the Deathfighter 7 and zipped past her window.

A second shot flew by my side.

At least they missed. Twice . . .

Casey pointed at the massive warship. Inching forward, it stalked us like an enormous metallic predator. "Move!" She put her hand on my bruised shoulder and gave me a good shove.

"Ow! Fine." Staring at the alien spacecraft, I slid out of the pilot's seat and made my way around to the other side.

Casey clambered right over the console, sat down and immediately began typing on the touchscreen keypad.

"I think they were warning shots," I said, settling into the copilot's seat. "What are you doing?"

"Trying to find out how to start the—"

"Warning." The computer had finished booting up. "Potentially hostile alien vessel. Full shield deployment is recommended."

"Oh, cool," Casey said. "It talks."

"Well, it's a little tricky. You have to talk to it the right way or—"

"Computer. Deploy shields," she said without hesitation.

Four loud clicks were followed by, "Shields deployed." My sister was pretty good at specific questions and commands. Especially commands. "Tell me how to start the engines."

"Would you like to access the Digital Pilot's Handbook?"

"Yep," Casey replied.

Welcome to the DPH appeared on the monitor, followed by a menu of choices. She typed in the second item from the list, *Initiate Propulsion System.* This became the title at the top of a screen jam-packed with tiny print.

I leaned over to see terms like *velocity management systems, plasma injector stabilization integrator* and *optimal thrust production.* I shook my head. *Great. More hopelessly confusing information from the computer.*

My sister studied the data, even grunting the odd "uh huh" or "okay."

"Casey, what are you doing?"

She continued just as if I hadn't spoken, eyes fixed on the screen.

I glanced at the Deathfighter. It had come to a stop now, close enough that I could make out some details: vents, hatches and dark windows. I shuddered, realizing that aliens were probably staring right back out at us. "Casey!"

"Shhh. I'm reading." She tapped on the touch controls and the next page came up on the monitor.

"Nice try." I pointed at the screen. "But we both know there's no way you can read that!" I was a way better reader than she was, and even I had no idea what most of it meant.

She kept her eyes on the monitor. "Yeah, I kinda thought so too, but . . ." She leaned in closer to the screen. A few more seconds, and she moved on to the next page.

"Casey! You're wasting time! Those aliens aren't gonna wait around for you to—"

"Aha!" She sat up, then slid the speed control to the *Off* position. "Computer, initiate Emergency Propulsion Start-up Protocol."

"Safety restraints must be fastened in order to engage the propulsion system."

Casey found her seat belts—two straps on each side, making an X when fastened just below the chest—and buckled them up. I put mine on as well. Not that it would matter; we weren't going anywhere.

At least half of the lights on the control panel blinked on and the gauges all sprang to life. Then came a whirring sound from the rear of the cabin that rapidly increased in pitch before settling into a comfortable thrum.

"Emergency Propulsion Start-up Protocol initiated," said the computer.

"Yeah!" She pumped her fist.

What? "How did you—"

Two more shots sprang from the Deathfighter's blasters and slammed into the front of our ship.

Casey looked up briefly, brow furrowed, then turned her attention back to the complicated instructions in the pilot's manual.

"Forward shields at 52%."

"Casey. Let's go!"

"Still need to figure out how to fly this—"

The computer beeped, then spoke. "Message received from alien vessel."

My stomach flipped.

Casey looked up, pursed her lips, then refocused on the screen. "You wanna get that?"

"Uh . . ."

The computer asked, "Do you wish to have the message displayed on the monitor?"

"Nope," Casey said. "Reading."

Our electronic friend offered another option. "Message may be read aloud."

"Roger that, Computer," I said.

Casey glanced over, raised one eyebrow, then went back to her research.

"The message is as follows," the computer began. "Casimonian shuttle, your presence here is an act of war. Prepare to surrender your ship. Failure to comply will result in your immediate destruction."

9   Under Attack

Casey just kept on reading. Faster now, though. Just a few seconds per page.

My heart pounded. *How can she just sit there?* "Casey! We—"

Another beep. "New message received from alien vessel."

"Read it, Computer," I said.

"This communication includes complete instructions for your surrender. Begin by turning off power to—"

"Got it!" Casey sat up and slapped her thighs. "Computer, mute." She attacked the touchscreen controls, tapping and sliding her fingers. New displays popped up on the monitor—various brightly coloured readouts, questions and instructions.

"Casey, what are you doing? You're supposed to be—"

"Turning everything off?" She looked at me. "Right. So we can be taken over by aliens? I don't think so." More lights started flashing on the control panel. She flicked several toggle switches on the console and checked a couple gauges.

"But . . . you heard them." I took a breath to calm myself. "If you don't do what they say, they'll blow us up!"

"Mmm . . ." Her fingers were flying across the control screen. "Not if we're not here!" She took hold of the speed control and slid it to *Surge*.

The engines howled; our small craft jerked forward, hesitated, then shot straight at the Deathfighter 7.

"Aaaahh!" I cried.

Casey nudged the speed even higher. What was she doing? The massive ship filled the entire front window. We were about to crash into a starship twice the size of an ocean liner.

"Warning. Ten seconds until impact." A buzzer sounded: on, off, on, off. A large red light flashed on top of the control panel.

"Casey!"

No response. She was a statue, stoney eyes fixed on the Deathfighter.

This is insane! "Casey!" She didn't move. I had no choice. I dove for the speed control.

Casey's hand swung from the handle and thumped me in the chest, stopping me instantly. While I gasped for air, she withdrew her hand, edged the speed down, paused, then fingers flying, punched in a final command.

The nose of our ship dropped like a boulder off a cliff. My face and arms flew forward, then snapped back as the seat belts held my torso in place.

The view ahead was only stars. No Deathfighter. *Yes!* I couldn't believe it. "How did you—"

Before I could finish my thought, Casey took hold of the speed control and cranked it up to *Lightspeed*. What a feeling: like swallowing pure energy! But she didn't stop there. Her hand continued to slide the lever through level 2, then 3.

I remembered what happened when I tried to go to *Lightspeed 4*. "Whoa!" I had to yell over the roar of the engines. "Stop! You can't go past 3!"

She ignored me and I reached out to stop her, but she froze me with her death glare. Hand over my now-bruised chest, I held my breath as she took us all the way up to level 5: *Maximum Light*.

Acceleration. Vibration. The wailing engines. All of it building until it felt like we were riding a hurricane: bounced, buffeted and completely out of control. And then, all at once, calm. The eye of the storm. Just the gentle hum of the engines, and the stars streaking past in the silent blackness.

"Yes!" Another fist pump. She looked over and flashed her trademark grin: a little crooked, top teeth only, eyebrows raised. "You just need to read the directions."

I laughed and high-fived my sister. "That was awesome!"

"Thanks."

I wasn't about to say it out loud or anything, but I had to admit I was pretty glad to have her with me. I still had no idea how she'd been able to read all of that stuff the computer threw at her, unless . . .

"Do you think this is all because of Dad's machine?"

Casey's smile vanished. She paused, bit her lip. "Yeah, maybe." Her lips parted slightly, as if she wanted to say something, but then she just shrugged and shook her head.

I guess she hadn't really had any time to think about it; for her it was just show up, then save the day. I tried to help her out by answering the question she'd asked earlier. "I was watching the game show and I got bored, so I started to imagine I was flying a space shuttle."

"This one?"

"Yup."

"So, you think—"

"Warning. Alien vessel approaching. Time to intercept: 47 seconds."

"They're after us!" I cried. "Faster!"

Casey returned her attention to the monitor. "This is as fast as it goes. But—"

"Evasive maneuvers recommended," the computer said.

"Just what I was thinking." She set to work on the touchscreen.

Thump! Our little craft lurched forward. We'd been hit.

"Rear shields now at 77%."

She scanned some more complicated text on her monitor, then reached for a button on the control panel.

Another blast pounded the back of the ship.

"Rear shields now at 52%."

Two more impacts rocked the *Valiant*. Electricity crackled behind us, and I turned to see black smoke pouring from around the edges of an electrical panel at the back of the cabin.

"Warning. Rear shields are now offline. Emergency escape maneuvers recommended."

I spun and yelled, "Casey, go!"

"I can't!" She frantically flipped toggle switches and input commands into the computer.

The spaceship shuddered and the streaking stars once again became sparkling dots as we dropped out of lightspeed.

The stench of burning wire stung my nostrils. I looked over at Casey. "What are you doing?"

She continued her feverish work for a moment, then slammed both hands down on the control panel with a shout of frustration. The shuttle began to edge backward.

"What's going on?"

She blew out a long breath, then spoke slowly and deliberately. "They're pulling us in."

10 Fire

"What?" It came out like a question, but I'd heard her just fine.

"They have us! They're pulling us into—" A cough exploded from her lungs as smoke filled the cabin.

Right on cue, the computer broke in. "Warning: Environmental system compromised. Oxygen levels decreasing."

Casey pulled the collar of her shirt up over her nose, and forced out a question between her coughs. "Computer, where's . . . the fire ex . . . extinguisher?"

"Flame suppression canisters may be found at the rear of the cabin, panels C and H."

"Take over," she barked at me as she spun out of her chair and raced toward the smoking panel.

Take over? And do what? The smoke burned my eyes, sending tears streaming down my face. Pulling up my shirt, I stood up to make my way to the pilot's seat. A coughing fit overtook me and I dropped back into my chair.

I twisted around and squinted through smoke and watery eyes to see my sister—a shadow in the haze—step forward, stumble, then drop to the floor. "Computer!" I forced out the words, fighting for control of my burning lungs. "Gas masks."

A compartment popped open under the window beside each seat.

"Oxygen masks are now accessible."

I reached into the nearby cubby, feeling cloth and plastic. Yanking the thing out, I held it up: a clear mask with a stretchy fabric back, and a metal canister hanging from a short rubber tube. Prize in hand, I dropped to the floor and propped myself up against the wall with the apparatus on my lap. One hand still holding my shirt over my face, I worked with the other to find a button on the can. I pressed it, and hearing the hiss I'd hoped for, took a quick breath, then called to my sister.

She was less than two metres away, on her knees and elbows, hunched over and hacking violently. Hearing her name, she turned her head in my direction. I tossed the bundle toward her. The canister fell to the floor with a thunk, short of my target, but close enough for her to reach it. She grabbed it, fumbled with it for a few seconds, then pulled it over her head.

I rubbed my eyes with my sleeve and burst into another coughing fit. Casey yelled something, but it was garbled by her oxygen mask. Still on her hands and knees, she pointed at me, then at her face. She repeated herself, even louder, and slower this time. "Puh . . . yaw . . . maff . . . aw!" Again, she pointed; at me, then her face. "Yorr . . . mafk!"

My mask. Of course. I gave her a thumbs up, coughed, then clambered onto my seat, over the console and, lungs screaming, dove for the cubby that held the other mask.

I slid off the pilot's seat, falling head and shoulders onto the floor. I thrashed about until I was able to organize most of my body into a sitting position, with my back against the wall.

The smoke was getting thicker, even down near the floor. This time when I coughed, it felt like a knife tearing through my chest.

"Warning: Oxygen level critical."

I threw my arms blindly above my head, felt for the opening, and snatched the oxygen mask. Wrestling it over my head, I found the button and sucked in several breaths of much-needed clean air. There was a strap for the oxygen canister, which I wrapped around my midsection and velcroed tight.

Now for the aliens. I really didn't want to meet whoever was in that Deathfighter. I reached over and pulled myself into the pilot's seat. *Maybe I could—*

"Sima!"

Sima? Oh . . . my name. I struggled to my feet and turned to find my sister jogging toward me from the back of the cabin, holding what looked like a fire extinguisher.

I stepped forward to meet her. "What's wrong?"

"Oi . . . kann . . . terr . . . ii . . . odd!"

"What?"

She flipped up her mask just long enough to say, "I can't turn it on. It won't work!" She held up the red container, squeezed the lever, and nothing came out.

"Just use the other one."

"Wuh?"

I pointed to the other corner of the ship—panel H—and, through the cloud of smoke, saw a red canister on the floor that told me she'd already tried that.

She shoved the metal container into my hands. "Yuuphiggeridow!"

I squeezed the trigger. Nothing, of course. Spun it through my fingers, looking for a button of some kind. Nope. I pulled the trigger again. I shrugged, then extended my hand to return it to my sister.

Just as she reached for it, I noticed something. It looked like there might be a little silver button on top of the handle. I pressed it, then squeezed again. *Fshhhhhh!* A powerful spray of white powder shot all over Casey's new black sneakers.

Before she had a chance to react, the spacecraft lurched backwards, and we both stumbled. "What the . . . ?" I turned to look out the front window. There was nothing new to see,

56

but I could feel us accelerating more rapidly toward the enemy vessel.

Casey pointed to me, and then toward the back. Then at herself, and the front of the ship. It made sense; I had the fire extinguisher, and she knew how to operate the controls.

Heart thumping, I ventured into a cloud of smoke so thick I couldn't even see the back wall, except for a flickering orange glow. So, not just smoke now, fire. Three steps in, I guessed I was close enough, aimed at the flames, and shot. The blast of chemicals pushed enough smoke out of the way for me to see that I was too far away, and off-target left. I adjusted, steadied myself, and fired again. But at the exact moment I squeezed the trigger, there was a muted explosion in front of me that shook the whole ship.

A siren sounded and a flashing light caused the smoke that filled the cabin to alternate between red and grey. "Danger," the computer warned. "Reactor temperature reaching critical levels. Emergency measures must be undertaken immediately."

"Sima!" I couldn't see Casey and could barely hear her. "You okay?"

"Yeah!" I yelled.

The computer cut in. "Situation critical. One minute, forty-one seconds until reactor breach." I'd heard this before on *Space Journey*. It meant that we had about a minute and a half until we blew up.

I heard Casey say something to the computer. She was on it from her end; it was up to me to get it done back here.

The *Valiant* shifted again. I stumbled, reset my feet, took aim, and squeezed. *Fshhhhhht!* Nailed it. Flames out. But the smoke kept coming.

I squeezed the trigger again, holding it down this time, blasting the smoldering panel's half-melted plastic door, then tracing all the way around it. It was working! One more plume of smoke stubbornly streamed from the top corner. I stopped, took aim one last time, then let fly. *Fshhhhhhhhhhh!* A cloud of white powder surrounded the panel, but no smoke. "Yes!"

"Sima!" My sister's voice cut through both the siren and the pulsing red cloud of smoke. It still wasn't very loud, but I heard one thing clearly: fear.

I spun and raced forward, stopping just behind the seats where I could see through the haze and out the front window. What I saw stopped me cold. Dead ahead, stars. Below them, a black floor that stretched into a platform reaching 50 metres before dropping off into space. Above and to each side, our view was framed by rough, unpainted brown metal.

A heavy black metal door slid slowly down, shutting out the stars one by one, and sealing us inside the belly of the Deathfighter 7.

11 Out of the Fire, into the Frying Pan

"Danger," the computer warned. "Reactor breach in 1 minute, 15 seconds."

"What!" The fire was out! *Unless*—

The door—right side, near the back—popped open, and two gigantic bodies burst in through the pulsing haze, massive weapons leading the way. I raised my hands instinctively, but they charged us, yelling in a harsh, unfamiliar language.

The first grabbed me with his free hand and shoved me against the wall. The other pulled Casey out of the pilot's seat and tossed her to the deck. I was forced to the floor as well, where I scrambled as far forward as I could, my back pressed against the front of the cabin. My captor dropped to one knee, pointed his rifle at my chest, and yelled, *"Hakh'k na'tek!"* I got my first good look at his face. It was olive green.

Behind him, through the dissipating smoke, I saw two more aliens. One stood with his broad back to me, ducking to avoid hitting his head on the ceiling. He gestured and barked orders at the second, who swung a huge hammer at the damaged electrical panel, obliterating it. Tossing that tool to the ground, he reached for another—maybe a wrench?—in a utility belt that was slung around his waist. He wore a visor and, tapping the front of it, turned on a headlamp. With one hand he tore away a chunk of plastic to enlarge the hole he'd made. Then he peered into the gap and jammed his arm in up to the elbow.

"Danger: Reactor breach in 56 seconds."

I tensed, shifted.

My captor reacted immediately. *"Hakh'k dahg, hakh'k mikh'nahg."* The words escaped like a growl from between slightly parted lips that revealed two jagged rows of teeth. He shook his rifle and roared, *"Na'tek!"*

I froze, scarcely daring to breathe—almost *unable* to breathe.

A muffled yell came from the back. The alien digging in the panel—Visorface—slammed his free hand on the wall beside the hole. The smoke was flowing again. He pulled back a moment and hacked violently.

60

His boss roared a command. *"Dja'sh'k! Hakh'k na'pekh, trrikkit breex'nixch't'ahng trroolaht!"*

Another cough was followed by a short, angry response. *"Bekh!"*

Bossman stepped forward, his face inches from the other's visor. *"Hakh'k ja'kah'mikh'ja t'k?"*

Visorface, in spite of being the smaller of the two, did not flinch. *"T'k xahg'daht hakh'k ja'kah'mikh'ja."* He threw his wrench to the floor, and pointed at the hole. *"Kahk'pakht. Hakh'k ch'n'kaht vik, agzsh'k't'kaw!"*

Bossman took another step, pinning Visorface to the wall with his powerful chest. *"Hakh'k m'kiti pakka'tuuk!"* Even the siren couldn't drown out his mighty roar. *"Kiti kekh'maash! T'k—!"*

"J'bok! Shah'k'tang sss'k sh'bekh." My guard, yelling back over his shoulder, joined the argument.

"Danger: Reactor breach in 22 seconds."

"Are you insane!" Casey now. "Just fix the—"

"Na'ghaht, kiti'k!" her guard screamed, poking her chest with the muzzle of his rifle and silencing her. *"D'at'na'tahk t'k hxah'k'tang, t'k tahn'nahg hakh'k sh'k ch'n'kaht vik t'k'sha!"*

Bossman spun around to face us, raised his gun and pointed it, first at Casey's side of the ship, then mine. *"Pekh'vik!"* he boomed. *"T'k na'krroo na'nikh'da sh'mahg'tet hakh'k sh'da—"*

"10 . . . 9 . . . 8 . . ."

"Hxa-a-ahh!" A great cry from Visorface stopped everyone short. *"T'k kuh'k'tahg tuh'lagh!"* Then he dove back

into the hole, hands first, followed by his head, his broad shoulders straining at the already-enlarged opening.

We froze.

"... 4 ... 3 ... 2—"

"Grr-aaagh!" The alien's left arm flew from the hole, clutching a chunk of plastic and metal with wires dangling from each end.

"Reactor offline. Core stable."

I sucked in a breath, closed my eyes, blew it out.

Visorface withdrew himself from the hole, thrust the critical component into the air, threw back his head, and let out a mighty roar. Then, with a nod to his boss, cast it to the deck, picked up his hammer, and strode out the door.

Bossman grunted, mumbled something under his breath, then barked a brief order at the other two soldiers before exiting.

"*Baxa!*" A powerful olive green hand grabbed my shirt at the chest and effortlessly pulled me to my feet. "*Tuh'lagh!*" With his gun he motioned for me to move to the door. I glanced back to see Casey stumble as her guard shoved her into the cargo area. My guy seized my shoulder, pressed his gun into the middle of my back, and hurried me to the exit. "*Na'daw'tek. Ah'tekh.*"

I stopped short in the doorway. We were in a massive, dimly-lit hangar. Awaiting us were five more Gamnilians standing in a semi-circle four metres from the door. They were gigantic: tall—pro-basketball tall—and muscular, but lean. The only one not pointing a large black rifle at me was

Bossman, who stood slightly off from the rest, frowning, gun casually tucked under his arm.

A sharp jab in the back forced me out of the ship. I hopped the half metre from the shuttle floor to the hangar deck, and took a step to regain my balance. The soldier at my back gave me a shove and I stumbled, falling facedown at the feet of the waiting guards. In seconds, Casey landed right beside me. A glance told me she was okay. Not injured, at least.

I pushed up onto my elbows and found myself staring at a pair of green Gamnilian feet more than twice as long as my own, though not much wider. No shoes. And each foot had only four toes, the eight yellow toenails much like human ones at their base, but ending in a slightly hooked point, almost like a claw.

I slid my knee forward, shifting up onto my left hip, and lifted my eyes. First, the stretchy material of the snug brown uniform that covered the soldier's long, muscular legs. A thick black belt around a waist almost as slim as my own. Bulky, black body armour moulded to the shape of washboard abs and powerful chest and shoulder muscles. And, of course, the enormous black gun—some sort of blaster.

Then the face. It was long and narrow like the body it belonged to, with heavy cheekbones and a bony ridge above each tiny coal-black eye. And no hair—not even eyebrows—but another ridge crowning the skull, adding several more centimetres to his towering height.

Two more Gamnilians stood on each side. Same uniforms. Same lean, muscular frames. Expressions ranging from sneers to stone-faced loathing.

"F'kiti'k," said the one in the middle with a smirk.

The others chuckled.

"F'kiti'ka'makh," he added.

They all roared with laughter, sounding like jackals with whooping cough.

"V'tik." The shrill voice came from behind them, stopping their laughter. The semicircle opened up to make way for a new member.

This one was smaller than the others and wore a blue uniform with a bronze, V-shaped sash. *"Kiti'tek t'an! Shah akht!"* He spoke quickly, one hand at his side, the other waving about for emphasis.

The rest of the group shuffled two steps back and resumed their stance, rifles trained on us.

Mister Bluesuit stepped forward. He looked down on us, then up at the two guards behind—the ones who had taken us from our ship. "This is it?"

He spoke English!

"Yes sir," they responded.

Huh. Them too.

"Children?"

"Yes sir." Their voices were far deeper than their commanding officer's.

"No others?" He tilted his head.

"No sir."

He turned his attention back to us and motioned impatiently for us to rise. "Stand up."

We obeyed, taking a couple steps back as we did so. While he was definitely shorter than the other Gamnilians, he was still taller than most humans.

"What are you doing here?"

I had no idea how to answer that question. I looked at Casey. She opened her mouth, but nothing came out.

"Do you not speak the language of your own people?" *He knew we were from Earth?*

I nodded. "Yes . . ."

"Then answer my question, Casimonian."

Wait. No. Casimonians speak English. It was all so much to process. I tried to think of a way to answer him, but I didn't even know where to start.

He wasn't prepared to wait. "I see. You refuse to talk. Typical! Our people go to the trouble of learning your language, yet you still show us disrespect!" He threw his hands in the air. "You think you can hide your secrets? Casimonian fools! Perhaps I should have my soldiers kill you here and now!" The longer he spoke, the more high-pitched his voice became. "You should already be dead. You know that, don't you? Surely even little children can understand that no one survives against the flagship of the Gamnilian Empire without a little help."

He abruptly turned and paced to the rear of our ship, calling over his shoulder, "Bring them!"

The two guards behind us grabbed us and marched us just past the *Valiant*. Bluesuit pointed at the back of our shuttle, a mess of charred, melted metal. A thick, foul-smelling, greenish-grey liquid dripped off its surface and pooled on the floor below, making it look like someone had spilled a large, nasty milkshake.

Little Boy Blue started up again. "Our sensors told us you were nearing full reactor meltdown. In my opinion, we shouldn't have brought you in. Too risky!" More hand waving. "The back of your vessel caught fire as soon as we disengaged our environmental shielding. If we hadn't sent in our crew, you'd both be dead. We risked our lives for two Casimonian children!" He spoke so quickly that he was barely understandable. "You're lucky the commodore is merciful. *I* would've let you die; you deserved it!" He pointed at two bulky green tanks that lay nearby. "We emptied two full fire extinguishers on your pathetic little ship. 'A waste of resources,' I said!"

He paused for all of two seconds. "What? Nothing to say? How about *thank you*? Would that be so difficult?"

I swallowed. "Thank you," I managed. *For saving us from the damage you caused*, I wanted to add.

He folded his arms across his chest and I noticed his body armour, while still forming the shape of rock-hard abs, was perched upon a little bit of a paunch.

"Excellent!" he said to me before focusing on Casey. "I didn't hear *you*, though."

I held my breath. One, two seconds.

"Thank you," Casey mumbled.

Phew!

A smug smile spread across his thin green lips. "There," he said. "That wasn't so hard, was it? A little gratitude. It's the least you can do after all we've done for you, don't you think?" He returned his hands to his hips. "Now. Back to my question. What are you doing here?"

"But . . ." I sputtered. How could I possibly explain? "We . . ."

Casey had been staring at the floor. Suddenly, she raised her head, looked him in the eye and shouted, "We don't know!"

"Insolence!" cried the alien, his face several shades darker than when he had begun. His hands dropped to his sides and clenched into four-fingered fists. "Very well! I have done my best. You leave me no choice."

He turned to his men and threw up his hands. "Take them away! Perhaps a night in the brig will loosen their tongues."

Once again, two soldiers roughly took hold of us. Before they hauled us away, their commander left us with a final message. "In the morning, you will answer to the commodore himself. He knows how to deal with disobedient children."

12   Space Cadet

The lights dimmed, the white metal door on the far side of the room slid open, and two Gamnilians entered our five by five metre cell. The first, tall and lean, carried a covered plastic tray. "Come here," he said, as the door slipped closed behind them. His deep voice echoed against the metal walls.

The second, who held a rough cloth bag in one hand and a silver flask in the other, tapped his foot on the floor just in front of them. "Sit." He was the shortest alien we'd seen— perhaps only as tall as our dad—and definitely the widest, with a broad chest and potbelly.

Casey and I sat across from each other on two beds, which were the only pieces of furniture in the room. As we rose to our feet, I glanced at my sister, who eyed the guards suspiciously.

"Come!" said Wide-one, his voice taking on a dangerous edge.

Skinny stepped forward quickly, nudging his partner with his elbow as he pushed past. "It is good. We will not hurt you." He paused and raised the tray slightly. "Food for you." Then his mouth twitched. He was trying to smile.

I was really hungry. Besides, this guard did seem different from the others. I got up, took a few cautious steps, and sat at their feet. Casey followed reluctantly.

Skinny dropped to one knee, bowed, then placed the tray gracefully between us on the stainless steel floor. He slid his long olive fingers from the tray to the sides of the lid. *Tahk'makh,*" he said. "Special best Gamnilian food, just for you." He bowed again, then swiftly removed the lid, dramatically raising it above his head.

The stench flooded my nostrils like a tsunami of sewage and rotting fish. I gagged, hiding my face in the crook of my arm in a desperate attempt not to puke.

"Ugh!" Casey pulled back from the steaming pile and plugged her nose.

Reddish brown chunks—of meat?—sat atop a slimy bed of tangled, oozing tubes. These were about as thick as macaroni, hollow—mostly—and grey. All of this rested in a pool of thin black liquid.

The Gamnilians roared with laughter. Casey made a move to stand, but Wide-one dropped the flask, grasped the back of her neck and forced her back to the floor. Kneeling beside her, he plucked a piece of meat from the top. "*Djar'ba* bladder," he said. "Fresh!" He popped it in his mouth, biting down just as it passed between his sharp yellow teeth, causing brown juice to squirt out and dribble down his chin. He picked up another piece, holding it in front of Casey's face. "You eat."

Casey turned her head and struggled to shake off the Gamnilian's grip.

Wide-one laughed and took the meat for himself. "Maybe . . ." He reached down and pinched one of the tubes between his fingers. "Maybe you like this?" There was a slurping sound as he pulled a piece as long as my arm from the pile. "*Kha'bawk'naht* guts."

Skinny chimed in. "Intestines," he said with a wink. "Make you strong!"

His partner dangled it in front of Casey, who finally broke away, falling onto her side with the effort.

Wide-one looked at Skinny, pretending to be surprised. "She not like!" Then he turned and offered it to me. "You?"

I gagged again.

More laughs.

"We eat this way." He raised it well above his bald head, looked up, lowered it slowly, and when it reached his open mouth, snatched it between his lips and sucked. The tube slipped in like a gigantic, wriggling worm, sending a spray of slimy juices in all directions until the last little bit slapped against his chin, then disappeared between his thin lips.

He wiped his mouth with his arm, shook his head in mock disappointment, and rose to his feet. "Not hungry, maybe," he said to Skinny, who responded with a laugh. Tapping a button on his belt, the door slid open and he turned to leave.

Skinny called after him. *"J'bok!"*

Wide-one stopped in the doorway. *"Tuhg?"*

His partner pointed at the bag he held. *"Gikh."*

The stocky guard frowned. *"Ban'akh'tee?"*

"F'dawkh'k'tang. Khit'k meel makh mahg'tet khit'k."

Wide-one grunted and tossed the sack on the floor between us. Then he noticed the cylindrical flask he had dropped earlier, which had rolled near the door. Picking it up, he shot his buddy an evil little grin, then lobbed it to me. It took me by surprise, and I turned my head and raised my hands to block it. Bouncing off my forearm, it skittered across the floor as the two guards walked out, laughing.

* * *

Back on our beds, I choked down a bite of the dark brown bread that had been in the bag we were given. It was dry and bitter, but we hadn't eaten since lunch with the relatives, which seemed like days ago now. I offered Casey the last piece.

"I'll pass," she said, holding up a hand. Her eyes were red. I'm sure mine were too; they'd been sore since the fire. "So . . . you were imagining flying a spaceship?" She made her "thinking face": knit brow, pursed lips and a slight frown.

I raised the bread to my lips, felt the grit still clinging to my tongue from the last bit, then tossed it on the floor. "Uh huh."

Casey looked down at the smooth, grey mattress she sat on; touched it. She rose to her feet, stepped over to the wall at the head of our beds and knocked on the white metal. "Feels real to me."

"Yeah." I nodded. "I know."

She turned and spread her arms. "So, what? You imagined it, and it actually happened?"

I shrugged. "Well . . ."

"That's crazy. You know that, right?"

"Pfff. Yeah!"

"So, what? You were daydreaming and—poof!—you were here?"

"No . . ." I took a moment to remember. "It was like any daydream at first. Then I was, like, 'Whoa, this is pretty cool; it almost seems real.'" I thought some more. "Then this guy started talking to me on the radio, and I didn't understand him. I thought, 'That's weird.'"

"Why didn't you stop? Or just imagine home?"

"I couldn't! I tried, but I was still in the ship."

"Huh." She thought for a few seconds, opened her mouth to say something else, but then a cough cut her off. She walked over and picked up the flask from where we had set it at the end of her bed. Unscrewing the lid, she raised it to her nose. "Can't smell anything . . ."

"*I'm* not drinking it." All of the smoke in the *Valiant* had made my throat dry too, but if what the Gamnilians drank was anything like what they ate, I wasn't interested.

"I'm thirsty." She took a sip. "I think it's just water." She drank a little more, then abruptly lowered the flask. "Hey! You should've just imagined you were the best space pilot ever: fly the ship, fight the aliens. Just like *Star Journey.*"

"*Space Journey.* And I tried that. It worked for awhile, but when I tried to go to Lightspeed 4 . . ." I rubbed my aching neck.

She shook her head. "Figures."

"What figures?"

"Let's face it, Simon: Only you could daydream your way into a spaceship—that you can't fly—that's about to be blown up by aliens."

"Hey, I—"

"The space cadet does it again!"

Space cadet. I hated that name. The first time she called me that was at school during recess in front of half the class. I didn't even know what it meant. "You know," she'd said, "someone who's always off in space daydreaming. Like *you* were when Mrs. Moffat asked you that question in Math class!" Naturally everybody laughed, because of course it was true. I'd looked like a complete idiot, and Mrs. Moffat got mad at me for not paying attention. Since then, the name had stuck.

"Well what was I gonna do? Sit around watching some dumb game show all day?" I did my best game show host impression. "Hey, folks! Today's big question: What chemicals are most commonly found inside . . . a *cow turd*?"

She rolled her eyes. "It'd just be nice if you tried living in the real world instead of hiding in your imagination."

"Right." I folded my arms. "Speaking of hiding, whose idea was it to go into Dad's room?"

Casey pressed her hand to her chest. "Oh!" she said in a high-pitched voice. "I'm Simon. I don't want to break the rules; I might get in trouble!"

"In trouble? What, like getting zapped in the head and trapped in outer space?"

My sister took a step toward me. "So this is all my fault? How was I supposed to know that was gonna happen?"

I stood and faced her. "Uh, the sign said 'DANGER!', Casey."

"Okay, let's talk about danger." She tossed the water container onto her bed and put her hands on her hips. "How was the ship when you arrived?"

"Uh . . . fine . . ."

"Everything worked properly? Engines? Computer? Shields?"

I could see where she was going with this, and I didn't like it.

She stepped out into into the open space past the beds. "So there's Simon, happy as can be, sailing along in his little spaceship. No danger. No problems." She continued to walk and talk. "Maybe a few unicorns? A rainbow?" She stopped abruptly and turned to face me. "And how long did it take you to mess that up?"

"Hey, I didn't do anything!"

"Exactly. You didn't do anything. So by the time I show up, it's a total mess. You—" She stopped suddenly, brow furrowed. "Wait! Is that how I got here? Did you imagine me here so I could rescue you?"

"No . . . I . . ."

"Are you kidding me! You screw everything up with your little daydream, and I'm supposed to just show up and fix everything?"

"That's not how it happened!" I threw up my hands. "You don't know; you weren't there!"

"Yeah, well I am now. Thanks." She coughed again, then shook her head. "I can't believe you. You make a mess, get into trouble, drag me into it; I *save* you, then you blame it all on me!"

I didn't know what to say. How could I explain what it was like to imagine flying through space—like I had a thousand times before—then suddenly finding out it's real . . . and that you're terrified. It's easy to be a hero when it's just make-believe.

"You wanted to talk about danger." She spread her hands wide. "Look around, Simon. *This* is danger. And we're here," she lowered her hands, then pointed at me, "because of you."

She paused to allow her last statement to sink in, and in that moment, the cauldron of emotion that had been swirling around deep inside of me rose to a full boil, then came bursting out. "Fine!" I threw my hands up. "You win. Whadda you want?" I looked my sister right in the eyes, daring her to respond. "Here, I'll say it: You're right. It's all my fault. I screwed up, and then you came along and saved the day. You're a hero, and I'm a loser, just like always."

Casey said nothing.

I dropped back onto my bed. "I don't get it. Everything was great and then . . ." I couldn't look at her. "I don't know. I got scared."

Casey's gym shoes squeaked on the metal floor as she walked over and sat back down on her bed. "Everyone gets scared, Simon."

"You don't."

There was a brief pause. I looked up just as she spoke. "Remember the fire? When I was on the floor coughing?"

I nodded.

"I couldn't breathe." It was her turn to look away, just for a second. "I was scared."

"Yeah. Me too."

"You gave me your mask."

I looked down.

"And the fire. You went back there and put it out. Doesn't sound like something a loser would do."

Huh. I hadn't thought about those parts. I raised my head. "Thanks."

"I don't know what's going on, Simon. I don't know how we got here, or how we're gonna get outta this. But if we're gonna make it, it's gonna be together."

And for the first time since the whole thing started, I felt like we had a chance.

13   Who's There?

The door hissed open, sucking some of the light out of our already gloomy cell, but this time no one entered.

Casey stood.

I sat up on my bed. "What are you doing?"

"This is our chance, Simon!" She stepped toward the open door. The hallway was dark except for a slight red glow down near the floor.

"Casey," I said, the cold fist of fear clutching at my throat, "don't."

She spun. "Why not?" It was more of a challenge than a question.

"Maybe it's a trap." No, it was more than that. I could feel it: A thick dread sat in a pit deep in my gut.

"A trap?" A tiny smile bent her lips. "How do you know? Is there a *Danger* sign?" She laughed lightly, turned, and took another step.

"No! Casey, you don't know what's out there."

Again she spun. "Neither do you, Simon! But you're afraid anyway." She shrugged. "You're always afraid."

Movement behind her caught my eye. Just a flicker. For a moment, I thought I imagined it. "Your stupid imagination is your problem," Casey was saying. I squinted. There it was! A thin, grey tentacle slithered along the floor from the hallway, winding its way across the cold steel, inching toward my sister's right foot.

I opened my mouth to yell a warning. But all that came out was a strangled whisper.

She was still talking. ". . . and when there *is* danger—actual, real-life danger—you freeze!"

The snake-like arm slipped up the back of her sneaker, over the hem of her blue jeans, then disappeared briefly behind her leg. I summoned all of my will to force out a warning cry, a sound, anything. But again, only a hoarse whisper.

The tentacle peeked around her leg, edged forward, then suddenly coiled around her ankle. She looked down, eyes wide, and instinctively shook her leg. The creature pulled, snapping her foot to the floor and slightly backward. Off balance, Casey attempted to kick her foot forward, but the beast wouldn't allow it, jerking her whole leg back again, sending her falling onto her hands.

She looked up, her face a picture of horror. "Simon!" she called. But before I could react, another greasy limb whipped around her upper left arm, yanking it out from under her. She was on her stomach now, her one free arm reaching ahead, hand desperately trying to grip the smooth steel floor, but sliding hopelessly as the two tentacles—now a third, around her other ankle—tugged her slowly away. She called my name again, but this time it was cut short as another slimy rope wrapped itself around her face and across her mouth like a gag.

I willed myself to jump up and race to her side, to fight for her, with her, but I remained stuck to the bed, a statue.

Casey was thoroughly bound now, her cries muffled, her wide, terror-filled eyes the only visible parts of her upturned face. Panic rang out inside me like an alarm, bells, buzzers and sirens all raising the call to action, but still I remained frozen in place. Casey had almost disappeared from sight into the darkness. In my mind it was so clear, so easy—I could see myself springing to my feet, racing across the floor and tearing the tentacles off her—but my body? Paralyzed.

Casey's face was the only part of her that hadn't been dragged into darkness. She bit through the tentacle that cut across her mouth, spat out the flesh, then uttered one last cry. Not my name, not a word of any kind—just the terrified scream of a girl who knew she was about to die.

I jerked out of my frozen state, arms flailing, to find myself lying on my back in total darkness. It was only a dream.

I sat up on my bed, panting, scrambling to reorient myself. My head and heart were pounding. *Where am I?* Not even a sliver of light under the door, no windows. *Right. We're in a Gamnilian jail cell.* That part of the nightmare was true. My heart sunk. But we were fine, for now.

Lying back down on the hard mattress, I closed my eyes. I breathed in and out slowly to relax myself. It had taken me forever to fall asleep the first time; it didn't seem likely that it would be easier now. Not that I wasn't exhausted after everything we'd been through. But my whole body hurt from bouncing around in the ship earlier, my eyes burned, my head ached, and every time I almost fell asleep, a little cough would pop out to wake me up. Then I'd remember where I was, and what our little blue-suited "friend" had said: *In the morning, you will answer to the commodore himself. He knows how to deal with disobedient children.*

As Casey slept, the familiar, rhythmic sound of her breathing brought me some comfort. When the lights went off, she'd muttered to herself for a few minutes—she'd been trying to come up with escape plans—but fell asleep soon after. I tried to sync my breaths with hers, and eventually began to relax. Finally, I felt my mind go fuzzy around the edges as I began to slip into sleep.

A tapping sound echoed in the blackness.

"What?" Casey's voice, groggy and annoyed.

I sat up. "You heard it too?" I whispered.

She just grunted.

"Casey!" I hissed. "The tapping; we should—"

"It's nothing," she mumbled. "Go to sleep."

Tap, tap, tap.

"See!" I cried. "I told you!"

I heard movement on Casey's bed. "What're you doing?" she asked.

"Shhh! It wasn't me!"

Pause. "What was it then?" she whispered.

"I don't know."

"It was me." The small voice came from above us, somewhere between our beds.

For a moment there was complete silence.

Casey was first to speak. "Who's there?" She was trying to sound brave, but I could hear the fear in her voice.

"I . . . am Geet," came the soft reply.

"What do you want?"

Geet responded with the last thing either one of us expected to hear: "Please help me."

"Why do you want *our* help?" Casey asked.

"I . . . am like you. I want . . . to be free."

"And you want *us* to help you? We can't even— " Casey stopped suddenly. "Hey, are you in the vent?" When we were looking for ways to escape, we'd noticed an air vent high up on the wall between our beds. It was the only way out of the cell aside from the door, but was far too high for us to reach it.

"Yes," Geet answered.

Casey's response came quickly. "How'd you get there?" It was like she was interrogating the poor creature. He— she?—*it* sounded pretty harmless to me, but I couldn't blame Casey for playing it safe. It didn't sound dangerous, but this could all be another Gamnilian trick.

Geet replied, "It . . . is complicated."

"Who are you, anyway?" Casey demanded. "You're one of *them*, aren't you?"

"No," Geet said. "I . . . am one of . . . me."

Chuckling to myself, I asked, "Are you a prisoner too?" I waited for an answer, but didn't get one.

"Hey!" Casey called. Nothing.

I tried again. "Geet?"

No response. As we sat in silence, I strained to hear anything that might give a clue as to what our visitor was up to, or even if it was still there.

"You think it left?" Casey whispered.

"I don't hear anything."

"Probably a spy," she said. "Went to report back to the Gamnilians."

"Yeah, maybe." *Report what?* And this Geet sounded more like a good guy than a bad guy.

"Or it didn't like all the questions," Casey said. "Thought we were on to him."

"Do you think—"

A blinding flash of light cut me off mid-sentence. I froze, my heart pounding like a jackhammer. Casey popped up into a crouch on her bed, hands up in her best yellow-belt karate stance. She looked like a cornered animal—terrified, yet ready to pounce.

After a few seconds of high-alert silence, we realized what had happened: Someone had turned on the lights.

Casey awkwardly raised her hands into a stretch above her head as she stood up, then touched her toes and hopped down onto the floor. "Ah," she said, maintaining the act. "Okay. Ready to roll!"

"Don't forget your jumping jacks." I grinned.

"What?" She looked over, her face serious at first, but finally cracking as she realized she'd been busted. "Hey, gotta do my morning exercises!"

"It is not morning."

Casey looked up at the air vent. I sprang up onto my hands and knees and turned my face in the same direction. The metal grate was gone, and I caught a glimpse of movement in the darkness beyond the opening. Then nothing, until a coil of black rope shot out of the hole and unravelled itself. No sooner had the bottom of it hit the floor than we saw Geet emerge from the opening feet first and climb nimbly down the rope.

14 Geet

In a matter of seconds, he stood before us. Crouching with his back against the wall and his tiny hands half hiding his face, he looked like a squirrel about to nibble a morsel of food. His skin was caramel, and the biggest brown eyes you could possibly imagine on such a small person flitted back and forth between us.

"Hello," I managed, dropping back on my haunches. "I'm Simon. This is my sister Casey."

He slowly lowered his hands, revealing fine elf-like features: high cheekbones, narrow chin, pointy ears and a tiny, turned up nose. "Hello."

I kept the conversation going so Casey wouldn't scare him off with her questions again. "We thought you left."

He dipped his head. "Yes . . . I . . ." His little voice seemed to come from his disorganized mop of dark brown hair. "I needed to . . . break in . . . so we could meet." He raised his face slowly. "You did not . . . trust me."

Of course he was right, but looking at him now, it was hard to imagine we were ever afraid of him. He was much shorter than we were. Even standing at his full height he would only be up to our shoulders. And the snug, stretchy material of his one-piece outfit—it even had feet, like a baby's sleeper—revealed a slim build. Not too terrifying.

Casey spoke up from where she stood at the foot of our beds. "How did you *break in*?" Her voice had lost its edge.

"I . . . turned off the alarm, then . . ." He held his hands in front of his chest, and the tiny fingers of one hand clutched at the bright blue fabric. ". . . removed the grate."

"Nice." Casey nodded her approval. "How'd you do all that?"

He shrugged, then looked down again. "I . . . have some tools."

And some skills. "Are you a prisoner too?" I asked.

Geet nodded slowly.

"Why do you need us to help you?" Casey asked. "If you can break in, why don't you just break out?"

The little alien began to fiddle with his fingers. "I can . . . escape. I can . . . get to a ship. But . . ." He hesitated a moment. "I do not . . . fly them." He looked up and gave an embarrassed little shrug. "Flying . . . frightens me."

Casey grinned. "Geet," she said, "I think we might make a pretty good team."

He smiled for just a second, then bit his lip and looked down at his hands.

"What's wrong?" I asked.

"There is . . . one more thing . . ." More fidgeting.

"What?" Casey asked.

"You must . . . take me home."

I hadn't thought about where we'd go once we escaped. It made sense that he'd want to go home; obviously it was what we wanted too.

"Yeah," Casey replied, her brow furrowing slightly. "I guess we can try."

Geet's head tilted as he first studied her face, then mine. "You . . . want to go home too."

I nodded.

He paused for just a moment before announcing, "I will help you." The first hint of a smile appeared on his lips. "We will help each other."

"All right," said Casey. "Let's do this." She stepped forward and looked up. "That's a pretty good climb." She glanced at me and flashed a grin. "You up for this, Simon?"

The little alien took hold of the rope. "No," he said. "We need . . . a plan."

It made sense; my sister did tend to act first and think later. I wondered how far it was to our shuttle, and how many guards we'd have to get past on the way. To be honest, I wasn't even sure we'd be able to get up the rope. "Good idea," I replied.

"Yeah, I guess." Casey bit her lip. "But how much time 'til morning? We need to get outta here before those guards come back."

Geet's little eyebrows dipped and his forehead creased. "A few hours, but—"

"Okay," Casey took a few steps to her right. She often paced while she thought. "So getting out won't be a problem." She stopped suddenly and turned back to Geet. "But how do we get to the ship?"

"I am sorry . . ." our new friend said, "but . . . for now, you must . . ." he raised clasped hands to his mouth and lowered his gaze, "stay here." His eyes flicked up to check our reaction, then dropped immediately.

"Stay here?" Like my sister, I wasn't crazy about waiting around for the Gamnilians to come back. "Why?"

He shrugged, and without looking up, said, "I . . . must go and prepare."

"Prepare what?" Casey was back to interrogation mode.

"As you said," he answered patiently, "we need a way to the ship."

"How long will it take you?" I asked.

"I . . . do not know. Maybe . . . a day? Maybe more?"

Casey threw up her hands. "What? They're taking us to the commodore!"

Geet nodded. "Yes. That is good."

"Good?" Her eyebrows popped up. "How's that good?"

"We will learn things," he said. "And it will give me time to . . . get everything ready."

"That's easy for you to say!" Casey walked back toward the center of the room. "You're not the one who's being dragged off to see some angry dude who wants to hurt you."

"I have already met him. When I first arrived. I have been here," a faraway look passed across Geet's face, "a long time." He stopped for a moment, as if remembering, adding, "He will not hurt you."

"How do you know that?" I asked. "It sounded like he's really mean."

"He . . . *is* mean."

"Then how do you know he won't hurt us?" Casey asked.

He let go of the rope and stepped forward. "I will not let him."

If the commodore was anywhere near as scary as the Gamnilians we had met so far, it was hard to imagine Geet being able to do much to protect us. Apparently Casey thought the same thing. "How? You can't come with us. And," she gestured toward the harmless-looking alien, "no offense, but what could you do if you did?"

A slow smile worked its way onto his face. "Sometimes it is . . . useful . . . to be small."

I looked up at the vent. He'd managed to break out of his cell and into ours. He obviously knew what he was doing.

Geet continued. "It is . . . the only way. We need time." For the first time he made direct eye contact, first with Casey, then me. "And information. Your job is . . . very important."

I trusted him. "I think he's right, Casey. We have to do this."

She was quiet for a moment. "What do we need to find out?"

He replied, "We must know . . . what he wants."

"What he wants?" Casey repeated. "From us? How do you know he wants something?"

"If he did not, he would have . . ." Geet shifted uncomfortably.

"What?" I asked.

"You are . . . alive."

There was a brief, uncomfortable silence. "Oh," I replied.

Casey sighed. She was never a fan of waiting, and didn't love having to depend on other people. But we didn't have a lot of options. "You've got our backs?" she asked him.

The little alien blinked, cocking his head like a puzzled pup.

I explained. "She means, *Do you promise to watch out for us?*"

"Oh, yes." He nodded enthusiastically. "I have . . . your backs. And your fronts!"

We laughed. I looked at Casey, who finally gave in. "Okay. I guess we have a deal."

Geet clapped his little hands. "Good!" he said. "Good. I will begin right away!" With that, he grabbed the rope and clambered up and into the vent before we even had a chance to respond.

15   Commodore Lusec

I jumped as a buzzer sounded. The shiny, black doors of the commodore's office slid apart, revealing a large room even darker than the hallways we had passed through on the way from our cell. A blood-red carpet covered the floor beneath various pieces of black furniture that blended in with the gloom. Across the chamber to our right stretched a wall that was simply one big window from end to end.

A blaster jabbed me between my shoulder blades. "Move!"

In spite of wobbly knees that threatened to collapse beneath me, I obeyed. I stumbled in alongside my sister, followed by our two guards and their boss in the blue uniform.

"Ah, Marshal Wamrud," said a deep, rich voice.

We spun toward the sound.

Over seven feet tall, he stood in the corner with his back to us, gazing out the window. "Let us have a look, shall we?" Then he turned to stroll along the wall that gave us all a spectacular view of the stars.

The officer in blue scurried forward. "Yes sir." he said, gesturing for the rest of us to follow. "Let's go!"

Nausea swirled in my stomach as the muzzle of a gun urged me ahead yet again. We followed Marshal Wamrud past a large black table to the center of the room, then toward the window, where the commodore now stood, his back to us once again. Three metres away from the gigantic Gamnilian, Wamrud stopped, ordering us to do likewise. He gave a quick bow. "The prisoners, sir."

The commodore turned around. The leathery skin on the well-defined ridges above his eyes lifted, but his face was otherwise expressionless. "Children, Wamrud." He sighed. "So disappointing."

"Yes sir. Just as I said, sir." Wamrud spoke quickly in his thin, irritating voice.

The alien's head tilted slightly atop his long neck. "One is *female*, Wamrud. I'm sure I would have remembered if you had said *that*." He pronounced every word distinctly, so that each became its own declaration.

"Is it?" Wamrud studied Casey for a moment. Her jaw was set and her eyes burned like blue flames. The marshal didn't appear to notice. He just shook his head. "It is so difficult to tell with these Casimonians, sir."

The commodore folded his heavily muscled arms.

The marshal continued. "I share your disappointment, sir. Such poor specimens are not even worthy of your presence! Of course, you will recall that *I* said we should not waste our time with them at all. But you, O mighty Commodore," here he gave a little bow, "in your great wisdom and mercy, brought them aboard, in spite of the risk. Some might say—"

"Wamrud," interrupted Lusec, his voice so much deeper and calmer than the marshal's.

"Yes, sir?"

"Shut up."

Wamrud bobbed his head and made a few little noises like what you might hear from an unhappy hen, but stopped talking immediately.

The commodore returned his gaze to us and, hands behind his back, stepped forward with perfect posture until he stood right in front of us. He wore a gold sash that made a V over his black body armour. The crimson uniform beneath stretched like a second skin over his sinewy muscles. "So it has come to this, has it?" he said, looking down his nose at us. "Now the pathetic Casimonians are sending their *children* to me."

I wasn't sure whether he expected a response. Even if I'd known what to say, I doubt I could've gotten the words out. I swallowed. Part of me wanted to poke him right in his beady little eyes, but of course that wasn't going to happen. So, along with Casey, I just kept staring up at him. My neck hurt.

"They are so quiet, Marshal Wamrud," he said after a moment.

The marshal stepped forward. "Yes sir. Exactly the same as yesterday, sir. When they first arrived, I—"

"You should be more like them."

Marshal Wamrud, lips flapping wordlessly, slid back into position beside us.

The commodore studied us briefly, then sighed. "I suppose you may be right, Wamrud."

The marshal straightened and opened his mouth to speak before being frozen by his commander's icy glare.

"Perhaps they are worthless after all." He was silent for several seconds, as if in thought. "But perhaps not. I think it is time we found out, don't you?" Then he spoke to the soldiers behind us, gesturing to the middle of the room. *"Pikh fjahg."*

They took hold of us and, grabbing a couple of black metal chairs, thrust us down onto them.

Lusec waited for the other Gamnilians to step back before speaking. "Comfy?" he asked.

We nodded.

"*Very* good," he said with a little bow, a fake smile pasted on his face. "You see, we may become friends yet."

I doubted it. But then I'm quite sure he did as well.

"Now then," he placed his arms behind his back, turned and took a few casual steps along the window. "Tell me why you were sent to attack my ship."

I blinked. Attack his ship? Did he think we were insane? Casey and I glanced at each other, but neither of us found the words to reply.

The commodore stopped in his tracks, turned and roared, "When I address you, you *will* respond!"

I jumped, and words spewed from my mouth in a jumbled mess. "We were—I mean, we—we *weren't* attacking you," I blabbered, "or your ship—or anything! Sir."

"I see." Lusec nodded thoughtfully, then resumed his calm pacing, back in the opposite direction now. "I have misjudged you. My apologies."

A sigh of relief shuddered through my body.

He stopped, smiling warmly. "No more assumptions. I shall allow you to explain." He raised his "eyebrows." A jagged scar sliced down the left side of his forehead, through the bony brow ridge, ending just below his eye. "So, what exactly *were* you doing?"

Of course, once again I had no idea how to answer his question. I looked at Casey, but her only response was a quick, frustrated shrug.

Lusec's eyes narrowed.

I had to say something; I decided to start at the beginning. "Uh . . . there was a game show on, but they were just talking about cows and stuff so . . ."

The commodore's head tilted slightly. "Cows . . . and stuff?"

Casey raised her eyebrows and mouthed, "What?"

Okay, fast forward. "Anyway, um . . . I was flying in a spaceship, and . . . this guy came on the radio and said I should go to . . . um . . . somewhere. I can't remember."

He took a step toward me and set his hands on his hips. "Can't remember? Or won't?"

"No, really, I . . . It was . . . a supply mission. He definitely said that. And not to attack the enem—the, uh . . . at least . . ."

The commodore shook his head. "Tsk, tsk." He dropped his hands to his side and stepped forward with the grace and power of a jungle cat stalking its prey. "Lying is *such* unbecoming behaviour for a commander in the noble Casimonian Defense Force." Standing in front of my chair now, he towered over me.

I shrunk down in my seat. "Commander?" I said. "I'm just . . . I'm not a commander . . ."

"Boy," he growled, "I do not enjoy games. I know the uniform of a Casimonian Defense Force commander when I see it."

I looked down at my clothing. Of course.

He turned his attention to Casey in her jeans and T-shirt.

"And this one then, Commander?" He nodded toward Casey. "I assume that this is your servant girl?"

I winced.

"Servant girl!" The dormant volcano had erupted.

"Oh. It speaks." The corners of Lusec's mouth turned up ever so slightly.

"I'm the pilot!" She leaned forward and pointed a thumb first at her chest, then at me. "And he's no commander—he's my brother. If it wasn't for me, we would've been dead a long time ago."

Commodore Lusec summoned another phony smile. "I see. How delightful." He stepped to the side so that he stood in front of my sister. "Now we're getting somewhere, aren't we? Perhaps, oh mighty pilot," he bowed with a flourish, "you will be the one to explain."

Casey raised clasped hands to her chest. "Well, I'm *just* a little *girl*," she said, her voice dripping honey and sarcasm, "but I'll try."

Lusec froze.

I cringed.

A slow smile spread across his thin lips. For several seconds, the only sound in the room was the ever-present hum of the airflow system. "You have moxie," he finally said. "I like that."

I let out the breath I'd been holding in.

"Very well." His smile vanished. "Tell me, *girl*: What are you doing here?"

Casey slouched down in her chair and shrugged. "Don't know."

Lusec slowly bent forward, sliding his hands down to his knees and leaning in, his green face just inches from hers. "I think perhaps you do not fully understand your situation."

Casey's eyes never left his even for a second. "I'm not afraid of you."

With a lightning-quick movement, Lusec grabbed Casey's forearm and twisted it, thrusting her to her knees at his feet.

She cried out, struggled briefly, then screamed, "Let me go!" in a voice that mixed anger, fear and pain.

Lusec stood over her, still gripping her arm, murder in his eyes. "Not afraid?" he boomed. "Then you are a fool."

When all she could manage was a whimper, he turned to me. "And what of you, *Commander*? Will you not courageously leap forward to save your dear sister?"

Looking at Casey in pain on the floor, unable to defend herself, I couldn't remember ever seeing her like that. Me, sure, but not her. I should have jumped up, yelled, attacked him—something. But I didn't. I couldn't. Instead, I went all fuzzy and numb inside and sat there with my mouth hanging open waiting for it to end. *Geet, where are you?*

The commodore paused long enough to ensure my complete humiliation. "No response? I thought not." A mocking smile spread across his thin lips. "Do not worry, boy." He looked down at Casey and sneered, "*Moxie* isn't everything," before pushing her to the floor and releasing his grip.

Casey grabbed her shoulder and winced, but continued to looked right at him, tears betraying the defiance that burned in her eyes.

Lusec shook his head, then stepped forward again, this time brushing right past my chair. "Bring them," he said to his soldiers.

"Yes sir!" came the eager response from behind us. "Get up! Let's go!" said the marshal, his voice like nails on a chalkboard.

I jumped up and leaned over to give Casey a hand, but she struggled to her feet on her own. The guards grabbed us, jerking us toward a darkened corner. There they once again made us sit down, this time before the commodore's massive ebony desk.

He sat in an enormous black metal chair, its back fanning out on either side of his head. "Light," he said, and a lamp on the ceiling spilled its dim rays onto the desk, casting long shadows down his harsh face so that his eyes were invisible beneath his sharp brow ridges. "Do I believe that you are here to attack us? Of course not. Even the Casimonians," he spat out the word like poison, "would not be so stupid as to send two children in a cargo shuttle to engage the flagship of the Gamnilian Empire."

He leaned forward, laying one of his large hands atop the other. The lamp illuminated the ridge than ran from the top of his forehead back over the crown of his skull, bony spikes spaced out every few centimetres along it. "But you *are* here for a reason. I believe you both know exactly what it is, yet you choose to keep that information from me." He raised his hands, resting on his elbows now. "Very few choose to resist me. Particularly ones as small and weak as yourselves." One strong hand rested over top of the other, which was clenched in a fist. "You are fortunate. I might well have killed you where you sat."

He leaned back again. "But you have information that I want, and when I want something, I get it." Looking up at his marshal, he said, "Wamrud, take them to the Doctor."

16 Doctor Appointment

We rounded a corner into a dim hallway, maybe ten metres long, leading to a single door. A dead end. The only sound was the soft echo of our footsteps as we marched toward our interrogator.

The door slid open as Wamrud approached. Stepping aside, he gestured toward the entrance, saying with a smirk, "Time for your check-up, children." With the encouragement of two blasters at our backs, we stepped into the room. The door slipped closed, shutting out the chuckling of the three Gamnilians.

The room, twice the size of our cell, was well-lit—especially compared to the rest of the ship—and the brightness assaulted our eyes. You'd think more light would make it less frightening, but no. It just allowed us to see everything more clearly: every silver machine, every black tube, every high voltage cable, every shiny hook and sharp needle. Every implement that it made very clear how the Doctor went about his business. And off to one side, near the far left corner of the cluttered laboratory, stood two stainless steel tables, silently awaiting their next victims. Us.

Casey wrinkled her nose. "You smell that?" she whispered.

I nodded.

"Smells like the boys' washroom at school."

She was right. Sometimes kids would forget to flush the toilets. That was the smell. Faint, but unmistakable.

She scanned the area. "I think . . ." She looked over her shoulder at the closed white door. ". . . we're alone."

Keeping my voice down, just in case, I looked around. "Yeah . . ." Across the room, near the end of the wall to our right, stood a silver machine the size and shape of a refrigerator, but with a computer screen, flashing lights and dozens of buttons and levers. I couldn't see what was on the other side of it, but looking above it I was able to make out the top of a second entrance to the room. "See that door? What about in there?"

"The Doctor? Yeah, maybe." She grabbed my elbow and pulled me off to one side, farther from the mystery door and behind a metal cart covered with a variety of gadgets. "This is our chance."

"Chance?"

"To get outta here!"

"What about Geet?" I asked.

"Exactly. What *about* Geet? He was supposed to have our backs. *I* haven't seen him. Have you?"

I glanced up and spotted an air vent.

She followed my gaze. "Not there, is he?"

Of course, I'd also wondered why he hadn't shown up. But he'd promised to watch out for us, and I trusted him. "He wouldn't ditch us."

She shrugged and looked around the room. "But here we are."

"Hey, if he's not here, there's gotta be a reason."

"Right. Maybe they captured him. Maybe he's . . . hurt."

Or worse. I didn't even want to think about it.

Casey stood next to a black rectangular machine that was about as tall as she was. At the top was something that looked like a high-tech microwave. A dark red liquid dripped from the bottom edge of the door. She pointed to it, then gestured to the many other unpleasant-looking contraptions spread around the room. "These aren't toys, Simon. We need to get outta here."

"Geet said he had stuff to get ready. He'll be here."

She picked up one of the devices from the nearby cart. It had a black rubber handle the size and shape of a flashlight and two thin steel tubes that ran parallel to each other for about the length of my forearm. These were joined at the end by a metallic V-shaped prong, its two ends charred. She held it up. "Be here when? Before or after the Doctor uses this on us? Simon—"

Across the room, the door hissed open.

We froze.

The first thing I saw was its eyes. Three of them. One primary eye, the size of a billiard ball, waggling on a dark purple stem—maybe 30 centimetres tall—that drooped at the top to allow it to look where it was going. Two other eyes, ping-pong ball-sized, on slightly smaller stems, one on each side of its head.

Except that it didn't really have a head. It glided past a cart that blocked my view, revealing that the eyes were perched upon a purple jelly-like body—about the height of one of those garbage cans you see in a park, and shaped like a cartoon ghost. No arms or legs even, unless you counted the thousands of tiny worm-like things that wiggled underneath it, propelling it smoothly across the floor.

The main eye turned and looked right at us.

Casey slowly returned the Zap-O-Matic to the cart.

The creature stopped. Its face was near the top of its body, and was just a long nose like a miniature elephant's trunk above a tiny, round mouth. When it spotted us, the snout lifted slightly, revealing a single twitching nostril. A thick, greenish liquid oozed from the hole, stretched into a long string, then dripped onto the floor.

"Uh . . ." Casey said. "Hi?"

The eye tilted, dipped, then eased forward a couple centimetres. It studied her for a few seconds, then turned away as its owner continued its odd little journey across the room. The nearest secondary eye took over prisoner surveillance.

Casey tried again to connect with our host. "Are you the Doctor?"

The alien stopped. Pivoted. The large eye blinked. The creature puckered its lips like a fish, squeezing its tiny mouth into a perfect circle. *"Pffffffffffffffffffffltt,"* it said, before adding, *"Ffffffffsssst."*

Fart sounds. Our host spoke in fart sounds.

Its trek carried on alongside a counter that ran along much of the far wall. When it neared the steel tables, it stopped at a workstation. With its back to us, two eyes surveyed a computer screen, along with a variety of instruments and electronic devices spread out around it. The third eye continued to stare us down.

My sister attempted another question. "Do you speak English—or, uh, Casimonian?"

The little eyeball dropped slightly and squinted, but apart from that, the being simply ignored us. The smell Casey had mentioned earlier was stronger now, and even though the creature was on the other side of the room, there was no doubt where it came from.

Casey thought for a moment, then tried something different. "I have a gun," she said calmly.

My jaw dropped. "Are you nuts!" I hissed.

She nodded toward the purple blob.

No reaction.

"It doesn't know what we're saying," she whispered. "This is our last chance. Let's do this."

"Do what?" I glanced at Eyeballs. That one eye was still freaking me out a little.

Casey's gaze darted to the cart, then back to me. "We need a distraction . . . Maybe a fight." She bit her lip. "Yeah. Push me."

"What?"

She glanced at the alien, who was still busy at the counter. "We'll get in a fight. Then when it comes over to break it up, you hit it and I'll grab the thing off the cart and zap it."

"What? No! Hey, Geet's gonna be here. Besides—"

She shoved me. "C'mon. Push me."

Eyeballs swung another eye in our direction.

"No, I told you—"

This time Casey drove the heels of both hands into my chest and I staggered back. "Do it, Simon!"

"Ow!" I said.

The purple alien spun around.

I pulled down on the bottom of my shirt to straighten my uniform. "Don't be stupid. It—"

Casey stepped forward, stomped on my toes, then said, "Come on, ya little chicken." She flung her hands apart and leaned forward. "Here. Free shot."

My left hand swung wide and swatted her face full force with a shocking *slap*! Casey's face snapped to the side, eyes wide. She blinked, shook her head, then blinked again.

Did I really just do that? Shock, rage, pride and fear shot off like fireworks inside me. I couldn't decide whether to run for my life or hit her again before she realized what had just happened.

In my indecision, Casey lunged, grabbing the front of my uniform in both hands and slamming me up against the wall. As I flailed pathetically against her attack, she shouted, "He's coming!"

Right. Eyeballs. The plan. He was almost on top of us. I grabbed Casey's shoulders and heaved her back in the direction she'd come. She launched herself dramatically through the air, then hit the floor as though she'd jumped from a moving train.

Eyeballs stopped less than an arm's length in front of me, its stench burrowing deep into my nostrils. Its main eye had followed Casey, and now leaned left to look down at her. The other two sat up high on their stems and stared me right in the eyes.

"Do it!" Casey yelled.

I summoned all my frustration and rage—at everything, from the guy barking nonsense at me in the *Valiant*, to being stuck in a daydream, to the bullying of the Gamnilians—and threw a mighty punch right into the middle of its body.

My fist slowed only slightly as it struck the creature's purple skin, as though I'd punched a plastic bag full of pudding. I felt almost no resistance until my hand and wrist had disappeared inside it. Then my fist slowed, stopped and shot back out like a rock from a slingshot, slamming my arm into the metal wall behind me. I crumpled to the floor, clutching my screaming elbow.

Having neutralized me, Eyeballs turned to Casey. She was up on her knees, hand on the Zap-O-Matic. The alien's tiny "feet" wriggled into action, setting it in motion. Fortunately for us, it didn't seem to be built for speed. There was no way it would get to her in time to stop her.

Casey gripped the handle and swung the device around, taking aim. Her thumb found a red button on the handgrip.

I wondered whether she could shoot it from there, or if she'd have to make contact before she could zap it.

I never found out. A purple arm shot out of Eyeballs' side and wrapped itself around Casey's wrist, shaking it violently. The Zap-O-Matic flew from her grasp, hit the wall behind her and clattered to the floor. As Casey knelt wide-eyed and empty-handed, the limb looped around her, scooped her up and retracted so that it held her tight against its squishy body.

The creature pivoted and made its way toward the steel tables, one of the secondary eyes keeping its focus on me. Casey howled and rained blows upon the squishy alien until another arm oozed out of it and immobilized her. Finally, a third limb emerged from its back, stretched to the counter, and scooped up a device that looked like a cellphone with a pen nib attached to the end. The arm doubled back, reaching around the rest of its body, and touched the instrument to her head.

She went limp.

17 Just Imagine

I reached for the joystick between my knees and eased it to the right, while my other hand flipped various toggle switches on the console between the two seats. As the *Valiant* banked to starboard, I glanced out the window at the almost colourless landscape below. Dirt. A few drab buildings off to one side. Just like the first two times.

It wasn't quite reality, but was somehow more than a dream. The colours were washed out and the sounds muted, but at the same time, there were way more details than any dream: I could see every switch and button clearly, and read every word on the computer screen. It was like an old movie playing inside my head, except I was one of the actors.

After the Doctor knocked Casey out, he laid her on one of the stainless steel tables. I was next. When I backed away, he just shot out an arm and scooped me up. Like Casey, I fought back, and just like her, it didn't matter. A second arm wrapped me up, the third lowered the device, and when it touched my forehead, it was lights out.

That's when the show started. At first, it was just a blurry jumble, snippets from my life, some familiar and others that I didn't know I'd remembered: a big black dog licking my nose as I sat on my tricycle, my first birthday party, our family opening presents last Christmas. Just moments, there and gone, like someone changing the channels of my life. But then it settled on one, its own little feature film—the one that began with Casey and I finding Dad's machine, and ended with the two of us stuck in outer space. It was almost like living it all over again, and there was nothing I could do to stop it.

It was replaying a second time now. The first one stopped when it got to the part where Casey showed up, then just went back to the beginning. So here I was again, just past the game show and lifting off from the surface of Zargon.

There was a beep, and the computer said, "Altitude: 500 metres."

"Roger that." Obediently I straightened out the ship and tapped the touchscreen controls. What choice did I have? I was just a character in this rerun of my life.

"Hello, Simon," said a familiar, gentle voice.

What? Geet? This wasn't right. We didn't meet him until way later. *I'm imagining it.* I ignored the voice and double-checked my flight plan.

"You do not have to do what it tells you to do." It was definitely Geet, and it sounded like he was in the other seat, beside me.

I wanted to look over at him, but instead focused on the joystick, robotically raising it back to an upright position, levelling the spacecraft. I was stuck in the replay.

Another beep. "Altitude: One thousand metres. Please prepare for transition to autopilot."

Geet spoke again. "You are in the Doctor's laboratory. He is . . . doing a brain probe. It scans your brainwaves and replays your memories."

So that was how Lusec planned to get his information. *Is he watching this right now?* I was embarrassed. Angry. But I lowered my hand to press the autopilot button, just as I had twice before.

"I have . . . disabled the Doctor and accessed the brain probe . . . to learn, so I can help. And, so we can talk. I . . . have a plan."

Disabled the Doctor? How? What did you learn? What's the plan? I tried to open my mouth to let the words out, but I

113

had no more control of my voice than I would have over an actor on TV. I was a prisoner in my own memory.

The computer repeated itself. "Please prepare for transition to autopilot." My hand had stopped halfway between the keypad and the button.

Huh. That didn't happen the first two times.

"Good." I could hear the smile in Geet's voice. "You see? Your mind is strong."

His encouragement made me want to believe it.

"Please prepare for transition to autopilot."

"Just ignore the memory," Geet said. "You can imagine whatever you want. Start with something simple. Put your hand on your lap."

I focused on my hand, concentrated, mustered all my will to move it over instead of ahead. It trembled, then edged toward the autopilot. *I can't!*

"You can do it, Simon," he said, as if in response. His voice was kind and calm. "Relax."

Easy for you to say—

"Breathe. Slowly, in . . . and out . . ."

I remembered the night before in the cell, listening to Casey as she slept.

Once my breathing slowed, Geet resumed the lesson. "Good. Now do not think. Just . . . imagine . . ."

I looked at my hand. It was still.

"Block out everything else. Just picture your hand moving over to your leg."

I focused on my hand and tried to "see" it gliding toward me, and away from the button. It twitched. Then it stopped. Frustration.

"Relax," Geet said patiently. "You are . . . trying . . . too much. Trust yourself. You do this all the time."

I took another calming breath.

"What do you do when you daydream?" he asked.

I go away. My imagination was my hiding place, where I went when I needed to escape, to shut out all the stress and the noise, to be alone.

I went there: my imagination, deep in my mind. *My mind.* Not the brain probe. Its sounds and images faded—I couldn't quite make them disappear—and I pictured my hand gliding to the left and dropping gently down onto my lap.

"Yay!" Geet said, and I heard him clap his hands. "You did it!"

His words snapped me back to the memory. I looked down at my lap. He was right.

Then my hand twitched.

I left the memory and went back. For me, imagining was like painting a picture, adding layers in small strokes until I had created my own little world. It was like that now, but so much faster than ever before. The shuttle came to life in my mind—the controls, the window and the stars beyond—more vivid than the memory, but still not quite reality.

After giving me a moment, Geet spoke. "Now we can talk." I pictured his golden brown face, his fine features, his large, dark eyes. "We must make plans." His lips moved to match his speech.

"Yes," I said, hearing the word as it came from my mouth. I could speak to him now, but I had so many questions I didn't know where to start. "Okay, but . . ." I turned up my hands and looked around.

As Geet explained, I visualized him seated beside me, just across the console. "I . . . recorded the memories from the brain probe—yours and Casey's—and played them back."

"What about Lusec?" I asked. "Isn't that the info he wanted?"

"The commodore is waiting for the Doctor's report. But," a tiny smile snuck across his lips, "he will not get it."

"What did you do to the Doctor?" I couldn't picture little Geet taking on that thing, with all those arms appearing out of nowhere.

"Do you remember the air vent?"

I nodded.

"I . . . released gas into the room. He is . . . unconscious." He read my expression. "Do not worry. It is safe for humans. Bombulans have very sensitive respiratory systems."

"So, Casey's okay?" The last I had seen her, she was out cold on the table.

"She is fine. She was scanned by the brain probe, like you. I already talked with her. She is awake now."

"Awake? What's she—"

A harsh voice interrupted us. "Control to Commander Andrews. Come in, Commander Andrews." I definitely remembered this guy.

"The memory is cutting back in," Geet said. I could no longer see him, but instead found myself staring at the controls in front of me. "You can turn it off."

I shook the memory from my head, then returned to the picture of Geet I had created earlier in my imagination. "Turn off the memory?"

"Yes . . . but first, the intercom."

I didn't remember a switch for that. I shifted my attention from Geet to the console, and as I tried to recall how it was all laid out, everything dimmed, as though I was looking through tinted glass. I was back in the memory again, just like that.

"Commander Andrews." Radio Guy again. "Do you read?"

"Just imagine," Geet said softly.

Right. I dove back in, took a breath, then began. It was getting easier: just shutting out all the distractions and slipping off into a daydream. *Okay, my imagination, my shuttle.* On the console I visualized a black button, about the size of dime. Across it in white letters, it said *MUTE.*

"Commander Andrews, this is—"

I pressed the button. For a moment it was quiet. Then the computer spoke up. "You are receiving a message from Control. Would you like the message displayed on the monitor?"

This time I managed to stay in my imagination. "No." I thought for a moment. "Computer, mute."

Sweet silence.

Geet grinned. "Good! You are learning."

Yet I still had so many questions. "How is this all working?"

"When the Doctor found the memories Lusec was looking for, it used the machine to stimulate your brain so that it replayed them."

"Like a movie."

"Yes." Geet nodded.

"But you weren't there, in the memories."

"No," said Geet. "I added my voice. I am recording myself. At first, only the audio went through. The memories controlled what you saw. But now the video is . . . feeding your imagination."

"Almost like you're here." *But where is here?* "So . . ." I thought for a moment. "This is all in my head?"

He laughed. "Humans say funny things." Then he was quiet for a moment. "It is complicated. The memory? Yes, of course. It is stored in your brain. What you see around you now? It is also in your brain, mostly in a different place."

"My imagination?"

"Yes."

It was crazy that it seemed so real. I nudged the joystick to the left, just to see what would happen. The *Valiant* banked to port. Geet sat up straight, eyes wide. "Right," I said, "you don't like flying. Sorry." I levelled out the ship. It was pretty cool to be able to control the shuttle again. It felt like it was the first time I'd been in control of anything for a while.

We flew on in silence for a few minutes while I tried to piece it all together in my poor, overloaded brain. The headache was back, big-time. "But . . . what about," I struggled to find the right words, "when we were in space, and the Gamnilians, and . . . all of it."

He paused a moment, then said gently, "That is real."

18   Reality Check

Those three little words rocked me. Casey and I had figured it was real—it had to be—but hearing Geet say it somehow forced me to deal with it.

For several seconds, I couldn't even think. I stared blankly at a thousand stars that blinked at me from the blackness beyond the front window. Stars I was imagining, that looked almost like the real stars in this real universe. That I imagined.

"Simon?"

I shook my head. "How? I mean . . . how can . . ." I turned to my new friend, hoping he could somehow help me make sense of all this.

"Your father's machine," he began. "Casey's memories showed me what she saw when she opened the door and looked inside. I believe it is a cellular development accelerator."

"What's that?"

"It is . . . for healing. No one has ever been able to make one, but I always believed it was possible. A short energy burst supercharges cells in an injured body part so it gets better faster. If you exercise it right away, it increases the effect."

"Uh . . ." I had no idea what any of this had to do with us being stuck in space.

"It is . . . not meant to be used on the brain. For . . . safety reasons."

Dad must have known: *DANGER!* But Casey went in anyway. So did I. I shifted uncomfortably in my seat, accidentally bumping the joystick. Our little craft rolled to starboard, throwing us both off balance.

Geet jumped. As I brought us back to level, he said, "Maybe . . . autopilot?" His voice quivered. "Sometimes it is best to . . . surrender control."

I pressed the button and the joystick went limp, then tucked itself away beneath the control panel.

Geet relaxed and resumed his explanation. "After you woke up, you watched television. There was a . . . what is it?" He cocked his head. "With questions . . ."

"The game show?"

"Yes. Casey joined in. She tried to think, to remember. She exercised parts of her brain that will improve her reasoning abilities."

"Dad's machine made her smarter?"

He hesitated. "There are many ways to be . . . smart. But it will help her learn and solve problems."

"The pilot's manual!"

"I do not understand."

"On the computer." I gestured toward the monitor. "She read the pilot's manual. It's how she learned to fly the ship."

"Yes. It would take most humans months to learn all of that. She is using her skills right now, looking for information on the Doctor's computer. I asked her to find out how to—"

"But . . ." I rose from my chair and stood beside it, with my back to the wall of the shuttle. "That doesn't explain how we got here, how all of this is real."

Geet took a moment before responding. "What did you do during the . . . game show?"

I shrugged. "I got bored, so I daydreamed. But . . ."

"You exercised the parts of your brain that control imagination."

"So . . ." I struggled to put the pieces together. "My imagination got stronger?"

"Much stronger."

"Strong enough to actually make a spaceship?"

"Yes."

I felt like my mind was about to explode. "But . . ." I had seen Casey learn to fly the *Valiant* in minutes, so there must be something to what he was saying. But it still seemed impossible. "What about the Gamnilians? I didn't imagine them!" *Right?*

"It is complicated . . . I will try to explain." Geet was quiet for a moment. "In your universe, the law of conservation of mass prevents—"

I held up my hands. "Whoa! What?"

"I am sorry. The law of conservation of mass states that matter cannot be created or destroyed. So when—"

"No." That wasn't the part that bothered me. "You said 'in my universe'. *My* universe?"

"Yes . . . there are . . . many universes."

"There are?"

"Yes. Very many."

"And . . . we're in a different one?"

"We are in . . . this one. Yours . . . is a different one."

Whoa. We were a long way from home. "But . . . how?"

"It is complicated."

"You say that a lot."

Now it was Geet's turn to stand. "You have many questions. But . . . we must hurry . . . I have a plan, but soon it will be too late."

"It's just . . ." I wandered back into the cargo area. "Yesterday I was a normal kid in a normal house with a normal family. Now . . ." I stopped and waved a hand at the almost real-looking interior of the imaginary shuttle that was a copy of a real shuttle that was created in my imagination, "Well, this *isn't* normal."

"I understand. It is very . . . difficult . . . for you," He stepped toward me. "I . . . learned many things from the brain probe. Once we are out of the Doctor's laboratory, I will answer your questions."

"Promise?"

"I promise."

I nodded. "What do we need to do?"

"Everyone has a job. I have almost finished my preparations. I just need to complete the . . . device I have been working on. Casey's part is to find important information on the Doctor's computer; she is doing that right now." He thought for a moment. "Also, she may have one more . . . task, if—"

"What do you need *me* to do?" I asked.

"It is time to learn to use your new abilities."

"You need me to imagine something?"

"Yes. To make something."

"So . . . like, a real thing, not just in my head?"

"Yes. It is very important. The plan will not work without it. But . . . you are ready."

I hoped he was right; it sounded like everything depended on it—on *me*.

"Soon I will turn off the brain probe. When you wake up, you will be on the Doctor's table. Just stay there. Remember what you have learned. Block everything out. Just relax and imagine."

"Okay." I pressed my lips together and nodded. If Geet said I was ready, then I was ready. "What do you need?" *Maybe a couple laser blasters? A hole in the wall?*

Geet replied in his gentle voice. "A pin."

What? "Sorry, I thought you said *a pin . . .*"

"Yes," Geet replied. "Do they not have . . . pins on your world?"

"Yeah . . ." I suddenly realized what he must be talking about. "Oh, like, for a grenade?"

"I do not know . . . *grenade.*"

"It's a little bomb," I explained, "for blowing things up."

"No, no!" He laughed. "For clothing. There are none on this ship."

"Oh," I said. "A pin."

What were we gonna do, make a dress for the commodore?

19   Mind into Matter

It was harder than it sounded. If I was at home in my room, just sitting on my bed with the door closed, it would've been a lot easier. But I was lying on a cold steel table in a laboratory full of distractions. The first couple of times I tried to picture a pin, I heard something—a computer beeping, or Casey tapping her finger on the counter behind me—and lost focus. Each time I managed to shake it off and start over.

It was my third try and I was almost there when I heard another sound off to my left. It was something I couldn't quite place. Sort of a buzz, but softer. I opened my eyes and pushed myself up onto one elbow. There, maybe three metres away, was the Doctor: snoring contentedly, all three eyes closed and drooping like dying flowers, a little puddle of ooze on the floor beneath its snout.

I looked back at Casey, who was lost in her research. I'd already tried talking to her, but all I got back were grunts. I laid back down, closed my eyes, and started over. I tried to picture a pin. *Why did Geet want a—Nope. Don't think.* I tried again. I started to imagine a pin, shiny and narrow, with a red plastic head. *Red, or another colour? Or did he mean one of those with a tiny metal head?* A computer beeped. Frustration!

I remembered Geet saying, "*Relax. You are . . . trying . . . too much.*" That was it. I saw his kind face in my memory, heard his soft voice and felt some of the tension melt away.

"Thanks," I said to the little friend who had come to life in my imagination. I was there again. The two of us stood in a circle of soft light in the center of an otherwise dark room.

He smiled, and his warm brown eyes evaporated whatever stress remained. "Sometimes it is best to . . . surrender control." His voice echoed slightly in the empty chamber.

"I thought Casey was the one with the control problem." I chuckled. "So, you want a pin."

"Yes. It is very important," Geet replied.

"With a plastic head?" I asked. "Or a metal one?"

He just tilted his head.

Of course he didn't know, because I didn't know and this was my imagination.

127

Casey was mumbling to herself. Geet faded.

I took a breath, then slid back into the conversation. "Sorry," I said. "Silly question."

"Trust yourself," he replied. "You do this all the time."

He was right. I slowly stretched out my left hand, palm open. There, in that room, with no one but Geet, it was easy to forget everything else, and just . . . imagine. Staring at the pink flesh of my hand, I pictured a pin, short, shiny and sharp, simply appearing.

My palm burned like fire. My eyes popped open and I jerked my hand back. The Doctor's lab. A faint *ting-a-ling* of metal on metal. I'd just heard a pin drop.

I checked my hand. Sure enough, it was empty, but a narrow red mark angled across it like a burn. I pushed myself to a sitting position, then gripped the edge of the table as I paused to allow a wave of dizziness to pass over me.

Within a few seconds, my head cleared and I dropped onto my feet, scanning the floor in the direction of the sound I'd heard. I was searching for a pin on a stainless steel floor; it was like looking for a needle in a haystack. I dropped to my hands and knees and began to scour the area centimetre by centimetre.

After a couple minutes, I'd worked my way well beyond the distance the pin was likely to have travelled. Frustrated, I turned, sat down and gazed back over my previous path. It had to be here somewhere. *Unless it just appeared in my mind.* I decided I'd go back and restart my search. If I couldn't find it, I'd have to get back up on the table and try again.

When I leaned over to push myself up, I caught a glint of silver just under the table I'd been lying on. The pin! I jumped up, raced over and dropped onto all fours. After several tries I managed to pinch it off the floor between the fingernails of my thumb and forefinger. I raised it above my head. "Yes!"

Casey glanced over her shoulder, raised her eyebrows and returned her attention to the computer monitor.

I sprang to my feet and scrambled to her side. "Casey, I did it!"

"Mmm," she mumbled, without looking away from the screen. "Good job."

"No, no." I waved my prized creation. "You don't understand. It's a pin!"

"Yup," she said, still reading. "A pin."

My arm dropped to my side. What did she think? That she was the only one with powers? With an important job to do? I punched her arm.

Her head spun and her eyes shot daggers. "What?"

"Geet says we need a pin, or we won't be able to get out of here."

She rolled her eyes. "Whatever. So find a pin. I have a job to do, Simon." She turned back to the computer.

"There aren't any on—" I began, but she wasn't listening. I thought about smacking her again, but then I looked down at the tiny weapon between my thumb and finger. I raised, aimed, and jabbed it into her shoulder.

"Aaah! What the . . . ?" She jumped to her feet, and we were nose to nose.

I had her attention. "There aren't any pins on the ship. So I made one. With my *mind*." I lifted my hand to reveal my creation.

It was gone.

20 Gone

Casey leaned in, examined my empty fingers for a few seconds, then looked up at me. "Wow. You even made it invisible." She straightened and flashed a thumbs-up. "Impressive." With an eye-roll, she returned to the computer.

"No, you don't understand!" I said. "It was there. I . . . I . . ."

Casey wasn't listening. She was back at work, if you could call it that. I mean, she was just reading. Somehow, she got the easy job.

"I made a pin! It was right here." I pointed to my still-clenched thumb and forefinger.

She was shutting me out.

I kept talking, as much to myself as to her. "I must've dropped it." I looked around, didn't see it, then crouched to check more closely. We needed that pin. And I didn't really want to start all over again.

Finding nothing, I dropped to my hands and knees and began to comb the surrounding area. Geet had said I was ready, but all I'd done then was make things in my head. The pin was the first thing I'd made in real life. *What if I did something wrong, and that's why it disappeared?* I crawled along the cold, hard floor. *What if this is all in my head? Maybe when I found the pin I was just—*

"Phbpbpbpbpbpbpbpbpbpbpbt."

"Ew. Casey did you—"

"ThlplplplplplplplplI."

I looked up. Froze.

Not two metres away, the Doctor was stirring. Two of its eyes were tightly shut, but one of the little ones, only half open, gazed lazily about.

Uh oh. "Casey . . ."

No response.

The eye spotted me. It blinked. *"Pppppt!"* This one was a high-pitched squeak. The other small eye popped open and swung around in my direction.

"Casey!"

"Yeah," she mumbled. "Pin. Atta boy."

The Doctor's tiny feet began to wiggle. He wobbled, then approached, before veering off course and stopping. The two eyes looked at each other, then back at me. It tried again, beginning by rotating its body to reorient itself. This resulted in a slow, 360-degree spin.

I smiled. It appeared that Farty McEyeballs was having a little trouble waking up. I took advantage of the opportunity, rose to my feet and backed away slowly. The Doctor wasn't spinning anymore, but it was swaying like a drunken pirate, and two of its eyes were wrapped around each other. I needed to get Casey's attention before it got ahold of itself.

I turned, took one step, then felt a familiar, cold grip on my wrist. A wave of stink hit me as the Doctor yanked my arm, spinning me around. I leaned back against it and tugged with all my strength. I broke free, falling backward onto the floor right behind my sister.

"Huh?" Casey was finally paying attention. She turned, looked down at me, then over at the Doctor.

Its arm had retracted. The two eyes struggled to disentangle themselves.

"It's awake." She grabbed my hand to help me to my feet. "Why didn't you tell me?"

I raised my eyebrows and opened my mouth to respond, but I didn't get the chance.

"Uh oh." Casey was looking at the Doctor. The big eye was now open, and our foe began to wobble toward us.

The computer beeped. Casey glanced over, leaving me to stare down the alien as it made its way along its winding, semi-conscious path.

"It's Geet," she said after taking a moment to read his message. "He says he has a way to stop it."

"Do it!"

"I can't." She tapped at the controls. "I lost him."

The Doctor lurched forward, turned sharply and crashed into the counter. A little arm popped out of the side of its head and swept several items off the countertop onto the floor. Then it swiveled, took a moment to steady itself, and resumed its course.

Casey tried a couple more times, then turned to me. "Distract it."

"What?"

"I need time to get Geet back again." She bit her lip, then pointed at the corner where we had tussled after first entering the room. "Go over there, and . . . throw something at it."

"What?" I repeated. It looked angry enough already.

Casey turned back to the computer. I was on my own. The Doctor approached, getting steadier by the second.

I dashed between the two steel tables and skidded to a halt at the cart with the Zap-O-Matic.

The Doctor had almost reached Casey, who was still frantically poking at the computer screen. I grabbed the one thing off the cart that looked like it might be easy to aim: a small sealed jar with an electric blue liquid in it. I hefted it; it sat in my hand like a baseball.

The Doctor's side bulged as it sent an arm toward my sister. I pulled back and let the jar fly.

I was never any good at baseball. The jar shattered when it hit the edge of the steel table, and there was an explosion—the liquid flashed white, then vaporized in a puff of silver smoke—sending out a spray of shards, one of which lodged itself in the back of the Doctor.

"F/////////////!" I didn't know farts could be angry. All three eyes swung around to glare at me.

"Got it!" I heard Casey shout as the Doctor advanced on me with surprising speed.

It swung wide around the steel tables, avoiding the rest of the glass, bounced off the wall, then recovered. I reached for the Zap-O-Matic.

"Ew!" Casey cried.

"What?"

"I'm not doin' that," she said, more to the computer than to me.

My fingers closed around the black, rubber handle. "Doing what?" I asked, but I didn't wait for a response. The Doctor bumped into a cart not two metres away, sending several instruments clattering to the floor. I held the Zap-O-Matic in front of me like a sword, a warning to my adversary.

The little villain froze. For a moment we sized each other up. My thumb found the button, rested on it. A little bulge appeared on its "chest," slowly growing, thinning, edging toward me.

I dropped the end of my weapon so that it pointed right at the oncoming arm.

It hesitated. Then shot forward.

I pressed the button and a yellow jolt of electricity crackled between the two prongs. The whole device shook, vibrations shooting through my hand and into my forearm. All my hair stood on end, and the smell of ozone flooded my nose.

The Doctor's arm snapped back into its body. Then all three of its eyes widened as my sister—who had taken advantage of our showdown to sneak in behind our enemy—looped her forearm around the three stems, swung her other arm around the creature's body, and thrust her forefinger right up into the oozing nostril in the middle of its snout.

It was like turning off a switch. The Doctor simply shut down. Its eyes closed, its body slumped and the second Casey withdrew her finger, it began to snore.

I lowered the Zap-O-Matic. Casey raised her finger, covered to the knuckle in glutinous green goo. "Gross!" She whipped her hand down toward the floor, snapping off a glob of snot. I jumped back, and the booger landed right where my right foot would have been. She wiped the rest on her jeans.

I shuddered, then looked at the sleeping Doctor. "*That's* what Geet told you to do?"

"Yup. Apparently Bombulans have very sensitive respiratory systems."

"I wonder why he didn't just pump more gas in?"

"He said it might've made us a little groggy," she replied. "I asked. Trust me."

"That was pretty disgusting." I set the Zap-O-Matic back down on the cart.

"Tell me about it." Casey stepped around the snoozing alien and nodded at the device. "So that was pretty cool. Did you actually zap it?"

"Nah, it pulled away."

"Too bad." She picked it up and looked at the blackened prongs. "Whoa. Whad'ya think would've happened?" She turned her head toward the alien, and I followed her gaze.

The Doctor was gone.

Casey raised the Zap-O-Matic, and we instinctively went back to back, scanning the room. Nothing.

The computer beeped, and we both jumped.

"I got it," Casey said. "Here," She handed me the weapon. "Cover me."

She sprinted for the workstation and I followed a few paces behind, head on a swivel, Zap-O-Matic at the ready. There was still no sign of the Doctor.

I stood on guard beside my sister, my back to the counter.

"It's Geet," she said.

"What's he say?"

"Just a sec." Her eyes darted across the screen. "Huh."

"What?"

Once again she tuned me out to concentrate on her reading. She'd left Geet's message and was flipping through pages of detailed information.

I gripped the handle with two hands; eyes darting back and forth from what Casey was doing to anywhere the Doctor might be hiding. "What'd Geet say?"

She flipped back to his message, double-checked it, then bit her lip. Poking the screen with her finger, she opened a window that looked like a control panel. She slid three sliders all the way to the top, typed something in, then held her finger over a red button that said *APPLY CHANGES*. "Okay, Geet," she said, sounding far from certain. And she pressed the button.

"What did you just do?"

She looked at the Zap-O-Matic. "You can put that down."

"Huh?" I just stared at her.

"Seriously. You should put it down." She pulled it from my hand and set it on the counter behind me.

The tingling started at the tips of my toes and fingers, and danced through my limbs. I looked at Casey. Her face was greenish black. Squinting, I realized that all the colours

138

in the room had inverted. I smelled toast. Then, from somewhere deep inside me, came something like a warm breeze gently blowing outward. I was there, and then, as if I'd been been blown away like powder on a puff of air, I was not.

21   Refuge

I peered through the gloom. Shadows. Or maybe nothing. A thrumming sound. I shrugged my shoulders; opened, then closed my fists. Raising my elbow, I drew a circle in the air with it. My body felt like a shirt I'd put on backward. I squirmed, hoping to get everything to fall into place, and lost my balance.

One of the shadows moved. "You will be okay," it said.

"Geet?"

"Yes," my little friend replied, taking me by the elbow. "Careful. There is—"

I stumbled again, dropping to one knee.

". . . a little step." He helped me stand up. "Here. You should sit."

I squinted in the direction he was steering me. A grey metal chair.

After guiding me into it, he said, "Stay there. Rest. You will feel better soon." Then he scurried off into the darkness.

Resting sounded pretty good. I leaned back and the chair wobbled. There wasn't much light in the room, but I was starting to be able to see a little more clearly. To my right, massive girders reinforced walls of rough, grey-brown metal. Ahead, huge army-green barrels, stacked on top of each other.

A flicker of—light? movement?—caught my eye. I tried to focus. Maybe five paces away, halfway to the barrels, was a contraption bolted to a girder. A banged-up metallic dome hung over a low platform, and between the two the air was distorted and wavy, like a mirage.

In the blur the ghostly silhouette of a person began to take shape—a hologram, I decided. But then the image resolved, gaining substance, until . . . *Casey? Yes.* She wiggled her fingers, picked up a foot, shook it, then lost her balance and plopped right down on the platform.

A teleporter? Just like *Space Journey.*

Geet rushed over to tend to Casey as he had done for me when I arrived.

I wobbled to my feet, shuffled over and sat on the floor beside them. Looking at Geet, crouched on the floor with his hand on Casey's shoulder, I said, "You . . . teleported us?"

"Yes," he replied without taking his eyes off my sister.

"Simon?" Her face was only an arm's length from my own, but she appeared to be straining, as if looking across a great distance.

"Yeah." I set my hand on her knee. "Right here."

"Good." She nodded, then blew out a breath. "Wow. That was . . . crazy."

"It is . . . an unpleasant experience," Geet said. "But you will feel bet—"

A muffled explosion cut him off, reverberating throughout my body, shaking up all the little bits that had only just settled back into place.

Casey closed her eyes. "Yes," she whispered.

Geet just smiled.

I looked from one to the other. "What's going on?"

"It was . . . part of the plan," Geet replied.

Casey mustered a grin. "We blew up the lab."

I tried to put the pieces together in my scrambled brain.

Geet, still in a funny crouch with his feet flat on the floor, rested his forearms on his knees. "Do you remember how I told you that Casey's job was to find information on the Doctor's computer?"

"Yeah. . ."

Casey chimed in. "He said, 'Find out what would make the brain probe overload.' I assumed it was so we *wouldn't* blow it up."

"The Gamnilians will think it was an accident," Geet explained. "They will think . . . you are . . ."

"Dead." Casey nodded her approval. "Nice."

I looked at my sister. "So, you—"

"Pbplpbpbpbpbpbpbpbpbppllpffft!"

"The Doctor?" I got up, looking all around at the barrels, the huge stacked crates, and in the corner behind us, two metal tables with computers and a hodgepodge of electronic equipment. "Where is he?" I didn't want another showdown with *him*.

"I teleported him, too." Geet pointed up.

I lifted my eyes to the reinforced metal ceiling five metres up.

"We are in a storage room," Geet said. "There is a shelf above us."

"So, he's up there in a crate, or a cage or something?" I asked.

"No . . ."

"What?" Casey pushed herself to her feet, looking up and around.

Geet told us there was very little chance that he would come down. "Listen," he said. We heard the murmur of its tiny feet on the steel above us. It seemed to be moving toward the edge. Pitter-patter. Stop. Pitter-patter. Stop. Pitter—

"Ththllthththththththththththththth!" There was rush of tiny footfalls in the opposite direction now, accompanied by bumping, scuffling and crashing as the Doctor raced across

our ceiling, apparently contacting numerous items along the way. Then, *"Ffllt! Ffllt! Ffllt! Fshshshshsh . . ."*

We both looked at Geet.

"Bombulans are afraid of heights," he explained. "It has . . . shut down again."

Casey and I laughed.

"We are safe here." Geet climbed to his feet.

"You said this is a storage room?" I asked. "What about the Gamnilians?"

"They never use this one. I have been coming here for . . . a long time." He gestured toward the corner of his little sanctuary, where a lamp spread soft yellow light on the tables and all their gadgetry. "It is where I do my work."

I looked around the space, noting that the walls and metal shelf above obviously extended beyond the stacked storage containers. "How big *is* this storeroom?"

"Very big." He smiled, his dark eyes each reflecting a tiny circle of warm light from the lamp. "Big rooms with large objects make good hiding places."

Casey smiled, then rubbed her eyes.

Geet's head tilted to one side. "How are you feeling?"

"I'm okay," she answered with a little shake of her head.

He looked hard at her, then me. "I am sorry. Teleportation is . . . difficult. And a brain probe in the same day!" He picked up the chair I'd sat on earlier, setting it down by another that was in the corner near the two tables.

"Sit down. Rest." Standing alongside the chairs, he extended his arm, waiting.

We both sank gratefully into our seats.

"Good." He nodded his approval. "Soon, I will come too." Then he scuttled off to a rickety old podium he'd salvaged that stood across from the teleporter. There he busied himself on the tablet that sat atop it.

I hadn't realized how tired I was until we sat down. Casey's red-rimmed eyes told me she felt the same. There was so much for us to talk about, yet neither of us said a word. Sometimes twins don't need to. All that mattered was that here, with Geet, we'd found a little refuge. We were safe. Casey closed her eyes, and I did the same. All was quiet, aside from the tappity-tap of Geet's little fingers on the computer. A wave of exhaustion washed over me.

Dozing off, I slipped into a dream—my parents, home—when a familiar thrum called me back. I opened my eyes to see Geet scurry from behind the podium and bend down in front of the low platform to collect the latest arrival. When he joined us in the little circle of light in the corner, I was able to see more clearly what my nose had told me was coming. "Lunch," he announced with a smile, bearing a tray with a silver pitcher and a steaming loaf of bread.

22   Breaking Bread

"That thing bakes bread?" Casey asked with a crooked grin.

"No," Geet replied, a slow smile spreading across his lips. "But the Gamnilians have a big oven in their kitchen." There was a box under the table filled with pieces of various gadgets. With his foot, Geet steered it to a spot on the floor in front of us and set the tray on top of it.

Casey leaned forward. "Is that how you got all this stuff?" She waved a hand at the least cluttered table, which held three computer monitors, along with several smaller devices.

"Yes." Geet found another box with a lid on it, pulled it over and sat down. "Gamnilian donations!" He giggled as he ripped a piece of bread off the loaf and handed it to me.

It looked similar to what we'd been given in prison, but fresh out of the oven, it was warm and soft. I tore off a chunk, passed it to Casey and took a bite. A little bitter, but I swallowed it greedily.

Casey pulled some off and shoved it in her mouth. "But how'd you get the stuff for the teleporter?" she asked through a mouthful of partly chewed bread. "Sneak out of your cell, and then . . . what? Break into their labs 'n stuff?"

Geet lowered the morsel he'd been nibbling on. "Yes," he replied. "Once I found a way to get out of my cell, I spent months exploring the ship. Then many more finding the parts I needed, storing them up here and building my first teleporter."

Casey still had the bread. I cleared my throat and wiggled my fingers, indicating that I wanted it back. She tugged off a huge hunk, handed me the rest, then crammed the whole wad in her mouth.

I accepted the quickly shrinking loaf, taking some more off before asking Geet, "How long have you been here?"

"Four hundred forty-two days."

Wow. We were only on day two.

He explained that he'd started by making a small teleporter before creating this one. The second had been especially helpful with the larger items, like furniture and computer monitors. His final step was to modify it so that he could teleport himself. He'd made a number of changes, but was stuck on the last one. "Once I got the pin from Simon, I—"

"What?" Then I understood. "You teleported that too!" I spun on Casey. "Ha! I told you!"

She rolled her eyes, then reached over and grabbed the bread from my hand. Turning to Geet, she asked, "So . . . why a pin?"

"I will show you," he replied, rising from where he sat on the box.

Casey set the loaf down on the tray and we followed Geet to the teleporter. I hadn't looked at it closely before, but I realized now what a junky-looking mishmash of equipment it was: control panels, computer circuits and bits of old furniture all thrown together. It was amazing that the thing even worked.

He stopped in front of the girder that had become the machine's spine. A black steel box was bolted to it, and he unclipped the lid. "There." He pointed to a spot near the bottom of the control box, below a mass of wires, breakers and computer chips. "Do you see it?" There was another much smaller box that held only three things: two tiny clamps, and between them, the charred grey remains of a pin.

"Cool." I leaned in for a closer look. "What does it do?"

"When teleporting organic matter," he said, "energy transfer must be very carefully modulated, paying particular attention to—"

"Whoa." I held up a hand. "Slow down." With a smirk, I added, "Casey might not understand."

"I am sorry." He thought for a moment. "I tried . . . different kinds of wire, but they did not work. I needed steel."

I nodded. "The pin."

"Yes. There is steel on the ship, of course, but to . . . melt it down and shape it—I did not have time."

"So," Casey said, "you just got Simon to make some."

"Well," Geet replied, "you cannot make something from nothing. Simon was lying on the Doctor's table when he imagined the pin. The steel was drawn from the table."

I looked at my palm, which still had a pink mark on it. "Why did it burn my hand?"

"The transfer caused the steel molecules to move very rapidly, generating—" He caught himself. "It . . . got hot. Next time you imagine something, do not make it touch you."

Next time . . . "So, what kinds of things can I imagine?"

"That is a good question. I think, once you learn to control it, you will be able to imagine many—" A computer beeped in the corner. Geet turned abruptly and hurried over to check it out.

"Many *what*? Geet?" My mind raced with possibilities. Body armour. Maybe a couple laser rifles? Or a giant robot to bust us out of here.

Casey shrugged. "Who knows, Simon? But I'm sure you'll come up with something awesome, like . . . maybe a paper clip." She patted me on the shoulder and turned to follow Geet.

"Hilarious," I replied, falling in behind her. "And what's your superpower again? Oh yeah. Reading."

"And blowing stuff up," she said without looking back. Then, arriving behind Geet as he stood tapping away at the touchpad below one of the monitors, she added, "Oh yeah, and flying spaceships. But, hey, anybody can do that, right?"

Ouch. Which reminded me of something I'd been wanting to ask our little friend. "Hey, Geet. How come I could fly the shuttle when I first got into space, but not after?"

For several seconds, he carried on as though I hadn't spoken, fingers busy managing an assortment of windows on the center screen, his eyes darting all the while to the displays on either side. One showed the layout of a spacecraft—the Deathfighter, I assumed—and the other played a grainy black and white video. It looked like our jail cell, but with only one bed. Nobody there.

"Everything okay?" Casey asked.

After a moment's hesitation, he turned to Casey. "Yes. It is fine." He glanced at the computers one last time, then turned to me. "I am sorry. I promised to answer your questions." He motioned to the two chairs, and we sat. Casey once again attacked the bread, while Geet settled back down on the box. "Simon, your imagination made the spaceship, but—"

"Maybe you can fly them," I said to Casey, then pointed to my head, "but I *make* them."

"Whatever," she mumbled, crumbs tumbling from her overfull mouth.

Geet just ignored us and carried on. "But because of the second law of thermo— Sorry. I will make this simple. It had to appear in a different universe."

"Wait." Casey held up her hands, one of which held the end of the loaf of bread. "What?"

He cocked his head. "I am sorry. What is your question?"

I looked at Geet. "I got this." Resting a hand on my sister's shoulder, I said, "Oh, Casey. You see, dear sister, there are many universes." I sighed. "Must I explain everything?"

She responded with a brief glare, followed by a kind offer. "Want some bread?" The final crust bounced off my nose.

Geet's little brow furrowed as he looked from one of us to the other. Then he simply continued. "When the shuttle appeared, a new universe began to form around it."

"The universe we're in right now," I said.

"Yes."

"And it's real?" Casey asked.

"Yes."

Casey shook her head. "I need a drink," she said, picking up the pitcher.

Geet rested his elbows on his knees so that he had to raise his eyes to look at me. "When you first arrived, it was mostly . . . in your head." He smiled. "But, as the universe grew around you . . . you lost control."

"So . . ." I took a moment to sort it through. "It went from imaginary . . . to real?"

He nodded.

"But," Casey set down the jug. "What about me?"

"I do not understand."

"Didn't he imagine me in after that? After he lost control?"

"Yes. Good question, Casey. I wondered about that also." His face showed genuine compassion as he looked at my sister. I felt a little guilty for mocking her; this was a lot to take in, and I'd had a head start during the brain probe.

"Simon," he asked, "in the shuttle, were you *trying* to make Casey appear?"

"No." I shook my head. "The Deathfighter was coming, and I just . . ."

"Just what?"

I returned to the memory. ". . . pictured her there, beside me."

"What else were you doing?"

"Nothing." I shrugged. "There was nothing I *could* do. I was just kind of in shock."

"So, it was quiet," he replied softly. "No distractions. And you pictured your twin, who you know so well."

I looked down at my hands, folded in my lap. "Yeah."

"And she appeared." He sat up. "After I watched your memory, I knew that was the secret to learning to use your," he smiled again, lightly, "superpower."

I matched Geet's posture. "Relax," I said, imitating his soft voice. "Do not think. Just . . . imagine."

He giggled.

The computer beeped again. Geet sprang to his feet and raced over to it, the two of us taking up positions on either side of him at the table. A light flashed on the map of the Deathfighter, inching steadily across the image.

"What is it?" I asked.

His only answer was to enter a command on the touchpad. The computer zoomed in on the floor plan, and the pulsing orange light seemed to pick up speed as it marched down what appeared to be a hallway. Geet turned his attention to the third monitor. The empty jail cell.

"Geet?"

No response. The flashing light continued its journey; the cell remained empty. Until the door burst open and two Gamnilian soldiers stormed inside, blasters drawn.

Finally Geet replied. "We must go. They know."

23   On the Path to Safety

"Know what?" Casey leaned in to get a better look at the screens. One of the soldiers grabbed the mattress off the bed with his free hand and tossed it against the wall as easily as if it was a throw pillow. The other Gamnilian tapped a button on his belt and began to speak.

"About what happened in the Doctor's laboratory." Geet turned, walked a few paces, then faced us again. "That you are still alive."

Casey straightened and angled herself toward us. "How would they know that?"

"No evidence of . . . remains."

"But they don't know where we are?" I asked.

He bent down and removed the lid from the box he'd been sitting on earlier. "Not yet."

What? "You said the Gamnilians never come up here."

Geet was rummaging through the container on the floor. "They have never had a reason. Now, they will be searching for us."

Casey watched the monitor as the two Gamnilians spoke briefly, then left. "Where *is* that?"

Geet pulled out a cigar-shaped instrument and thumbed a button on its side that made it buzz. "It is my cell."

She turned to Geet. "Why are they looking for you? They don't know you know us, do they?"

"They might know now," he walked over to a steel shelf unit that stood against the crates, scanning it as he spoke, "if they found evidence of some of my . . . computer modifications." The rack creaked as he pulled a black utility belt off the top.

"How long?" Casey asked. "'Til they find us?"

He shrugged. "I do not know." He plucked a couple more items from the shelves, including a ratty brown knapsack. "This will not be the first place they look."

"Okay." I glanced at the monitors. The light was no longer blinking, and the cell sat empty, its door ajar. "So we're safe."

"For now." Hands full, he scurried over and knelt down to set the objects on the floor near the open box. He looked up. "We are still prisoners. Just in a different place."

It was quiet for a moment, until Casey looked at me and said, "They'll find us eventually. We have to go." She turned to Geet, hands on her hips. "How do we get to the ship?"

He rose to his feet and scanned the room. "We must be careful. To avoid their patrols." He trotted over and knelt down right between us to look under the table, muttering, "Where is the other one?"

I understood what Geet and Casey were talking about, but this was the safest place we'd been since the whole crazy adventure started. I wasn't thrilled about leaving it only to run right into a Gamnilian search party. "So what do we do?" I asked. "I don't know about you guys, but I don't feel like spending the rest of my life in a Gamnilian jail cell."

Muffled clacking sounds rose from under the table as Geet scuffled through the gadgets there, some in boxes, some strewn about the floor. "They would not put us in prison again."

Casey raised her eyebrows. "They wouldn't?"

He came out from under the table, several gizmos in hand. "Not after this. They will be . . . very angry."

We were silent.

He deposited his treasures in the pile on the floor. "The commodore wants to know why you are here. He will not give up until he finds out."

I wondered, for just a moment, how he might try to get that information from us. Then I thought it might be better to think about something else.

Geet stood and joined us by the computers. "The Gamnilians want only one thing: to control the galaxy. And no Gamnilian is more desperate to do that than the commodore. He must not find out about your father's machine."

"I'm guessing he wouldn't use it to heal anyone," Casey said.

"No." Geet folded his hands. "He would not."

"But," I said, "it's in another universe. So he couldn't get it."

"I believe there is a way. To get it. And to get you home."

Home. There was nothing I wanted more. "Really? How?"

"It is compli—"

"Complicated, I know. But—"

"We must go." His words were both gentle and firm. "I am sorry, but it will take too long to explain. The longer we wait, the harder it will be to escape."

I opened my mouth to respond, but didn't know what it was that I needed to say.

Geet studied me for a moment. "It will be okay, Simon," he said.

Will it? Geet always had a plan, and he always came through. *So far.* We'd only met him . . . yesterday. *Wow.* It was hard to believe; we'd been through so much together already. And I trusted him. But *okay?* I wasn't sure about that. A lot had happened since we'd left home that hadn't been *okay.*

157

His gentle voice interrupted my thoughts. "Simon?"

Our eyes met for a second, then I looked down at the hard black floor.

"Sometimes," he said, "the path to safety leads . . . through danger."

I raised my head, then nodded slowly.

"So what's the plan?" Casey asked.

"I have gathered some of the things we will need." He glanced at his little collection of odds and ends. I will prepare the teleporter. Then—"

"We have to do *that* again?" Casey wrinkled her nose. "How does it even work?" But before Geet could reply, she held up her hands. "Y'know what? I don't even wanna know."

Geet picked up a few articles from the heap, including the scruffy bag, then turned for the machine that would send us who-knew-where.

The computer beeped.

"Casey," Geet called as he headed for the teleporter. "Check—"

"Got it." Her eyes scanned the monitors. She called to Geet. "The light's flashing again. In a different place."

"That is good, I think." He stood in front of the podium by the teleporter, tapping away at the tablet that sat upon it. "Where are they?"

"Uh . . . I dunno." She studied the map. "Can't read this writing. Is that Gamnilian?"

"Yes. Use the monitor on the right. It is showing my cell now, but there are other cameras. Flip through until you find them." For just a second Geet looked up from his preparations. "Simon, I am busy and we must hurry. Everything on the floor must go into the utility belt."

It obviously wasn't as important as Casey's job, but I was glad to have *something* to do. I walked over to the little mound, knelt down and picked up the belt. The first thing that caught my eye was a small device that looked like a square cellphone. When I tapped the screen, the display lit up and it beeped. I glanced up at Geet, who was too busy to notice. *Focus, Simon.* There were a couple of pouches where it might fit. I'd have to ask Geet where he wanted it.

"Whoa! Lookit 'em all." Casey leaned in close to the screen, then adjusted the zoom. She called over her shoulder to give Geet her report. "The shuttle bay."

"Good," he replied. "Just as I thought." He made a couple more changes, then looked up. "It is time. Come." He pointed to the teleporter. "Casey, you will go first."

She jogged over and stepped onto the platform while I stuffed the assorted contraptions from Geet's pile into random pockets on the belt. He'd figure it out.

Geet brought her the knapsack. "You will need this."

She lifted the flap and peeked inside. "Cool! What does it do?"

"You will create a little . . . distraction. So we can get to the shuttle."

"Nice! How—"

"We must go." He returned to the podium. "I will be sending you to a little room by the shuttle bay. I will tell you more later."

I fell in beside Geet and held out the utility belt.

He simply nodded to the floor. I bent over, set the belt down and heard the thrumming of the teleporter. When I stood up, Casey was already disappearing, the girder and all its wires showing through her ghostly body.

"You are next."

My stomach flipped. It was easier the first time, when I didn't know what was coming. This time I'd just seen my sister vanish into thin air.

"Take this," he said, handing me a grey plastic ring.

"Uh . . . thanks." Not nearly as cool as whatever was in Casey's bag, I guessed. "What is it?"

"Put it on." He gestured to the teleporter. "Please hurry."

I stepped onto the platform, then looked down at the drab little trinket in my palm. It was obviously too big for me, but I slid it onto the ring finger of my right hand anyway. It immediately contracted. Perfect fit. "Wha-a-at?"

"I will explain everything soon," Geet said, head bowed over the computer pad that controlled the teleporter.

I tensed, expecting him to zap me into oblivion at any moment. Several seconds passed. Then several more.

"I am sorry," Geet said. "I must get this right."

Yes. Please do. Standing there staring at Geet's tousled brown hair while he fiddled with the controls gave me too

160

much time to think. To imagine. What if he made a mistake? What if the machine broke before he could join us?

Wait. Who'll set the controls for Geet? "When you teleport yourself, do you just run over at the last second?" I remembered my dad trying to set the timer on the camera for family photos. Last Christmas it took three tries.

For a few seconds, he just kept working. Then he looked up and paused a moment before saying, "I cannot come with you. Not now."

"What! Why?"

"There is technology here that the Gamnilians must not find. This teleporter. Other things."

"But how will we—"

The computer beeped again. Not just once; over and over.

"Should I check—"

"There is no time." He glanced at the monitor. "They are are coming." He lowered his head and continued to make adjustments. "I will join you soon. The device on your finger is a communicator. I will send you a message with our meeting place." He tapped his tablet.

The tingling began.

"Geet!"

24 On Our Own

Four faint lights pulsed in the blackness like distant landing beacons. In a line: blue, blue, orange, blue. I shook my arms and head, hoping to jolt my innards back in sync with my skin. The result: skull-splitting pain and a series of thuds echoing in my eardrums. I cringed, closed my eyes, and started over. The orange light had joined the others, all blue now. I looked around, finding more blinking lights and the glow of a couple of computer readouts. "Casey?"

"Hey."

I lowered my eyes and squinted through the murk until I was able to make out her location: sitting on the floor in the corner of yet another dimly lit room. "Where are we?"

She looked up for just a moment, and the glimpse of her face felt like home. "Some kinda control room, I guess." Her attention then returned to something that glowed on her lap.

My vision began to clear, so I scanned the area, which was about the size of a bedroom. There was a heavy metal door in the middle of the wall behind me, and just past it at the other end of the room, a large machine hummed softly. That explained the smell of electricity and hot metal. Aside from that, just a bunch of control panels. It was like one of those mysterious rooms at school that you only got a peek at every once in a while when the caretaker left the door ajar.

"Huh?" For a moment Casey stared at the computer tablet she held against her raised knees. "This doesn't make any sense." She shook her head, then looked up. "Geet here yet?"

"Uh, no. He—"

"Guess I'll ask him when he gets here." Her eyes returned to the screen.

"He's not coming."

Her head snapped back up. "What?"

I shrugged. "He said he had to stay. That—"

"What? Why?"

"He doesn't want the Gamnilians to get the teleporter and stuff."

"When's he coming?"

"Don't know. He said he'd send a message." I held up my fist, then pointed to the ring. "On this."

She ran her hand down the back of her head and rubbed her neck. "Great. I have to figure this out myself."

I opened my hand and angled it so I could get my first good look at the little communicator. A raised glass circle sat where the stone would be in a regular ring. I pressed it, but nothing happened. Bringing it close to my lips, I said, "Hello?" Nothing. *Tap, tap, tap.* "Hello?"

"Whoa." Casey had found something interesting.

I crouched to get a better look at the tablet. "What?" I wobbled a little on the way down, dizzy from the teleporter. Reaching for the floor to steady myself, my hand landed on the rough fabric of the knapsack Geet had given Casey. Beside it was some kind of controller. The strange writing on it told me it was yet another item Geet had scavenged from the Gamnilians.

I picked it up. It looked a lot like the transmitter my neighbour's dad used for his drone. Geet had said she'd be creating a distraction. "Is this—"

"No way!" Casey looked at the black device in my hands, back to the screen, then up at me, a grin taking over the bottom half of her face.

"What? He gave you a drone? That's—"

"Nope. No drone. Better."

"What?"

"There's a whole hangar full of Gamnilian fighters on the other side of the ship." She nodded at the controller. "That'll fly one."

My jaw dropped. "*That's* the distraction?"

"Yup." She took the remote from my hand. "Come to Momma, baby."

My finger vibrated. For a second I thought I was being teleported again, but then realized it was the ring. There was a narrow gap between the glass and the grey plastic, and it glowed red. As soon as I looked at it, a beam of soft yellow light shot out from around the glass, projecting a little hologram above it.

"Geet?" I closed my hand into a fist and raised it up to where I could see him better. His image, the length of my index finger, floated two or three centimetres above the ring.

"Hello." His voice was hollow and a little fuzzy. "You are safe?"

"Yeah." I instinctively glanced over my shoulder, wondering what danger he might have expected for us. "What about you? Did the Gamnilians come?"

"No," he said, "but they are near."

"So you'll be here soon?"

"There are things I must do before I leave. But yes, soon." The movement of his lips didn't quite match his words.

"Good," I said. "Where are we meet—"

"Did Casey find the files for the remote control?"

"Yeah, Geet." She explored the device in her hands, comparing it with a diagram she'd pulled up on the computer. "I read 'em. Just checking out the controller now."

"Good," he replied. "Have you found the blasters yet?"

"Uh . . . yeah." She studied the remote. "I think so. The red button?"

Holo-Geet remained silent, suspended above the ring, arms limp at his sides, staring straight ahead.

"Geet?" I leaned in for a better look.

He just hung there, like a marionette whose puppeteer had gotten distracted.

"Geet? Are you okay?"

"Yes," he replied, his voice barely audible. There was the sound of movement, then he was back, and easier to hear. "I am sorry. We do not have much time. Casey, after you lift off, turn the fighter toward the hangar door and hover there. Do not worry if they shoot at you; the shields will protect you."

Casey raised the tablet to get a better look at the diagram. "Shields?"

Geet didn't seem to hear her. "There will be an invisible force field across the exit. You must shoot out the field generators. If you hit the control panel to the right of the door it will disable them. Then fly out as fast as you can and—"

"Into space? Nice!" She examined a schematic that showed the hangar. "How do I open the door?"

166

"One shot with the plasma torpedo should create a big enough opening." Geet's likeness went limp again for a moment. It wasn't live, I decided; just some kind of recorded image that only moved when he spoke. "Maybe two shots. Make sure—" Shrill beeping replaced his voice. "I must go." Muffled movement sounds. "Please hurry! We need the distraction very soo—"

The transmission ended with a crackle, followed by several seconds of static. The hologram hung briefly above my fist, then vanished.

"Geet?" No response. The ring's red circle of light winked out.

We were on our own.

25 Taking Control

"Where'd he go?" I'd tapped and called. I'd even taken off the ring to look for a hidden switch, some way to contact him. Nothing. Now I paced the floor. "It sounded like he was still in his hideout. What happened?"

Casey was still obsessed with the techno-gadgetry Geet had given her. Without looking up, she said, "I dunno. But I could really use his help." She moved the controller aside to look back at the tablet. "I'm still not sure about the—"

"What's wrong with you?" I threw up my hands.

She looked up to where I stood at the far end of the room. "What?"

"Geet's gone." I stepped toward her. "He said the Gamnilians were coming, then the computer beeped, then," I slashed my hand across my throat, "cut off. They have him, for all we know, and all you care about is your stupid toy."

"Toy?" Her face hardened. "What, like your cute little magic ring?"

I shot her a glare.

"All I know is the last thing he said was we need the distraction *fast*." Her eyes met mine and locked on. "I'm doing my *job*."

Which is cooler and more important than mine.

Who was I mad at? Casey? Yes. Geet? A little. For giving her the best job, or for leaving us? Maybe both. Either way, there wasn't much I could do about it. "Fine." I shuffled over and slid down the wall beside Casey. It felt good to sit down. My whole body ached. Teleporting was the worst.

Casey had set down the remote and was once again speeding through the files that explained how to use it. "Aah!" She stopped and looked at me. "Y'know what? Enough of this." She closed the document she was using and opened a program that simply showed a grey screen with a white frame around the edge. She handed me the computer. "Here. Hold this."

She grabbed the controller and stabbed a yellow button near the top, which lit up. Power on. Then she crossed her legs the way she did when she was gaming at home.

"You know what you're doing?" This wasn't a video game.

"Uh huh."

I was pretty sure she didn't.

She nodded at the computer on my lap. "That's the camera. Turn it on."

I tapped the screen and several buttons appeared along the right side of the display. I pressed the big green one in the middle, and the screen came to life, showing a hangar much like the one our shuttle was in.

"Let's see," Casey said.

I raised my knees and angled the screen to give her a better view.

She leaned in. "So that's what I'm flying. Cool."

The camera showed several fighters lined up along the far wall, maybe 30 metres away. I thumbed a button and it zoomed in. Gunmetal grey, they were small—two-seaters, probably—and sleek. The engines hugged the fuselage and the wings swept gracefully back from nose to tail. These things made the *Valiant* look like our mom's minivan.

Two Gamnilians in grey uniforms strolled into view from our left, walking right in front of the ships, talking casually. Their muffled voices echoed in the cavernous space. I hadn't realized we had audio.

Casey returned her attention to the unit in her hands. "Let's do this." She hit a green button.

Two open-mouthed Gamnilian faces swung in our direction in response to the low hum of the engines. One turned and yelled back in the direction they had come. The other tapped his belt, speaking sharply, his voice now

170

clearly audible—on the fighter's radio, I guessed. *"Chahkh'b'xahg'daht'nahg! Nee'xahg'daht kiti'hakh'k'sha tuh'lagh'-na'daw."*

The engine noise increased in both pitch and volume until their voices were completely drowned out. The second one was still tapping away, and though I couldn't hear him, it was obvious he was getting angrier by the second. I zoomed out to see more of our surroundings.

"Here we go." Casey nudged the left stick forward and the spacecraft shot straight up, leaving the Gamnilians gaping up at us. Just when I thought the ship would hit the rafters, she jerked it to a stop, lowered it a bit, bobbed 20 metres above the floor for a moment, then dropped it all the way back down. It bounced, a crunch of metal revealing that she'd annihilated the landing gear.

No, she did *not* know what she was doing. "Are you kidding me?" I said. I should've been the one at the controls. I was better at video games, and I'd watched Nick's dad fly his drone. I held out my hand. "Let me do it."

She carried on as if I wasn't even there. Typical Casey. Jaw set, she popped the fighter back up, this time managing to hold it just a little above the floor.

There was an explosion and the image of the hangar shook, then tilted right. We'd been hit. Casey lifted us up a little, then shoved both sticks to the left. The ship banked to port, revealing a Gamnilian soldier off in the corner, 40 metres away, with his rifle to his shoulder, ready for a second shot. Two of his comrades scrambled to join him.

"Shields!" I hollered. "Are they on?"

"Guess not." Casey jerked the craft up a bit higher. We heard another blast, but the stable image on the display told us it had missed.

"Turn 'em on!"

"Geet didn't say which button." She bought some time by dropping the fighter down again, then shooting it back up, higher. Two more shots missed their target. She bit her lip, then jabbed a black button. Two parallel bursts of orange light flew from either side of the fighter, scorching the far wall. She raised her eyebrows. "Not that one." There were two buttons left. "Red or blue?" she asked.

I couldn't take it anymore. Geet was counting on us, and Casey obviously had no idea what she was doing. I made a grab for the controller.

Casey elbowed me away and jabbed the blue button just as we were hit again. There was a muffled explosion; the image flickered and shuddered, but remained stable. "It's the blue one," she said.

I shook my head. "Lucky guess."

In the corner, a door flew open and three more Gamnilians raced into the hangar. At the same time, the original soldiers fired off a series of bursts. Casey reacted and the ship dodged to starboard. Three blasts flew past, but two others hit their mark.

A message appeared at the top of the screen: SHIELDS AT 91%.

"Look." I pointed at the screen. "Let's go. We need to save our shields."

"Yeah, yeah." She eased the fighter backward, away from our attackers, who now fired freely. A few shots missed, but several did not.

"Come on, faster," I said.

"This is harder than it looks, okay?" she replied as yet another discharge thumped the shields. She poked the left stick ahead and the spacecraft jumped up, then she attempted a maneuver with both sticks that plunged the vessel toward a number of fighters parked off to our left.

"Look out!"

She overcorrected and our little craft swept back the other way, Gamnilian weapons firing all around us.

"The door's behind us." I said. "Turn!"

"That's what I was *trying* to do." Casey was wrestling with the controller now, as though she could steer the ship by moving it around. Her next move swung the nose to port. As it passed the soldiers below, her thumb poked the black button, letting off two blasts that obliterated some shelving, sending its contents cascading down on our foes.

But our spaceship, now completely turned around, was drifting. She managed to keep it from dropping onto the other ships, but as it ran along the front of them, the starboard wing clipped three, smashing their front windows. Then it dipped left, wobbled as Casey fought for control, and finally skidded along the floor, coming to rest 20 metres from the massive black door at the end of the fighter bay.

"Aaaah!" she screamed in frustration, then jammed the black button again, sending half a dozen orange bursts uselessly into the force field that blocked our exit.

"Wait!" I'd noticed something. "Do it again."

"What?"

"The blasters. Fire again."

"There's a shield," she said, but let off a shot anyway. As soon as she pressed the button, a little white box appeared briefly on my screen, like a target. At the same time, one of the buttons lit up.

The sound of Gamnilian shouting grew nearer. The image on my computer shook once, twice.

SHIELDS AT 67%.

"Go!" I said. "Buy me some time."

The engines whined as Casey jabbed the left stick, shooting the craft up almost to the ceiling. "What're you doing?"

"I think the computer aims the guns," I answered. Pressing the button that lit up earlier, the targeting box reappeared, holding steady in the middle of the screen.

She nodded as she maneuvered the ship so that it darted from side to side. Two Gamnilian blasts flew past and exploded into the rafters. "So we can knock out the shields."

"Yep." I just had to figure out how it worked. "Take another shot."

She fired. This time, the two orange streaks met at the exact spot where the white box hovered over the rough metal wall, leaving a huge black scorch mark. "Is that good?"

"Sort of . . ." I just needed to figure out how to move the targeting box.

The fighter was struck two more times. Casey jerked the fighter right, then left. "I can't do this forever, Simon."

There was only one button that I hadn't tried. I pressed it, and the image on the display was replaced by a completely new one: the view behind the ship.

"Whoa," Casey said. Then, "Hey, good idea." She pulled back on the right stick and the spacecraft shot to the back of the hangar.

I switched to the front camera just in time to see the cluster of soldiers in the middle of the room spin as one, then raise their rifles once again. "Simon, you've got about ten seconds." Then she resumed the little dance she'd been doing earlier, bobbing to and fro, Gamnilian weapons discharging all around us.

I touched the screen and the targeting box slid across the display, settling beneath my finger. "That's it!"

"You got it?" Casey asked as another explosion shook the fighter.

SHIELDS AT 56%.

"Yes. Go!"

She adjusted the spaceship so that it was back up near the ceiling, and directly in line with the door at the far end of the hangar, almost 200 metres away. "Here goes . . ."

She shoved the right stick all the way forward and the ship shot ahead. Then, as she adjusted the left stick, it swooped down until it raced along just above the floor. The flabbergasted Gamnilians held firm briefly, rifles at their shoulders, before scattering like mice at the sight of a cat.

I scanned the area to the right of the massive black door, and my eyes locked onto a rectangular panel. When I placed my finger on it, the box slid into place. "Fire!"

Casey punched the black button and two orange bursts flew to our target and destroyed it in a spray of white and blue sparks. "Yes!"

I couldn't join her celebration. *The door.* What did Geet say? *Some kind of cannon.* But I didn't know how to switch the targeting for that. The huge hunk of metal filled our viewscreen, blocking out all hope of a successful mission. All I could think of was how we'd let Geet down.

Then, milliseconds from impact, a fiery ball of destruction slammed into the door, blasting a hole dead center just in time for our little fighter to slip out and into open space.

"Huh," Casey said, before allowing herself a grin. "*That's* what the red button does."

26 Crash and Burn

"Now what?" With all the excitement over, reality set in: Our fighter was flying off into space without us, leaving us behind in a dark room somewhere in a Gamnilian Deathfighter. Still prisoners, just in a different place.

"Yeah. Good question." Casey glanced at the computer on my lap, which showed a familiar scene: blackness dotted with millions of points of light.

I switched to the rear camera. The Deathfighter was getting smaller. So far, no one was following. "Do we keep going, or . . . ?"

"I dunno. We did our job, right? A distraction." For now, she pushed the little ship onward, continuing to create distance between it and the Gamnilians.

"Yup. Big one." I smiled, switching cameras. "Can you imagine the commodore's reaction when he finds out?"

Casey grinned. "I'm sure he's heard." She readjusted herself so that she leaned against the wall with her legs stretched out in front of her. "So, he thinks we're all on that thing, right?"

Except maybe Geet. What if they had him? I didn't want to think about it, so I just nodded.

"So that'll make it easier to get to the shuttle. That's what Geet—"

My finger buzzed. My hand flew up from where it sat on the floor and made a fist in front of my face. "Geet! Are you okay? Where are you?"

His hologram sprung to life. "I do not have much time." He was whispering, and the connection was fuzzy. "You must listen."

I raised the ring to my ear so I could hear better, and Casey leaned in on the other side of it.

"Simon, there is some data I will send to your ring. It is a map of the top level of the Deathfi—" His holo flickered along with his voice. "—asey, you must fly the fighter back and crash it into the place I marked on the map. Simon will show you."

"Cool!" Casey said.

"Where are we meeting you?" I asked.

Static garbled the beginning of his response. "—are already at the meeting place. Where you are now is very close to the shuttle bay. When you open the door, there will be a hallway, and then another do—" The signal cut out again. "—through that, and your ship is to the left."

Casey spoke up. "But you'll be here, right?"

"I must go. The—"

"Geet," Casey said, "you're gonna meet us, right?"

"As soon as you crash the fighter, it will be time. You must go to—"

"You didn't answer my question."

"As soon as I finish, I will come . . . but if I am late, you *must* go to the shuttle. Do not—"

"Late?" I said.

"We're not leaving without you," Casey added.

His hologram flickered, and the transmission began to crackle, making it difficult to hear what he said next. "—*kck xxxcckkxxx*—after—*xck kkkkxxx*—delete this data—*kxx ksssxck*—ery important—*chxxxx kck*—come—*xxc*—promise —*xxc kxxxxxx*—not wai—*xch ckk*—be too late—" And after a few more seconds of static, Holo-Geet disappeared and we were left in silence.

As I lowered the ring, a shadow of concern passed over Casey's face.

It rattled me; worrying was *my* job. "What did he say? Something about deleting data?"

Casey nodded. "He must still be at the hideout."

"But last time he said the Gamnilians were close. He's gotta get outta there."

"Maybe that's what this new mission is about—buying him some time." In a heartbeat, her worried expression was replaced by a much more familiar one: fierce determination. She picked up the controller. "Let's go crash a fighter."

I took a breath, swallowing my fears, then let it out, blowing away all of my questions about Geet's safety. "Yup." I raised my knees and adjusted the computer so we could both see it.

Casey swung the spacecraft around, once again giving us a view of the distant Deathfighter. Two little dots had appeared, and were growing. They were after us. "Showtime." A trace of a smile turned up the corners of her mouth as she sent our craft racing directly at the enemy.

I looked down at the screen, watching the two Gamnilian fighters bear down on our ship as it rushed headlong into danger. Then stopped.

"What are you doing?" I asked.

"Waiting. Don't worry. They can't hit us from there."

Two orange flashes sprung from one of the oncoming vessels and sailed past us.

"Waiting for what?"

Four more bursts. The image flickered as one made contact.

"That." She dropped the fighter straight down 50 metres and jammed the right stick forward.

Several blasts flew harmlessly above our craft, followed by the ships that shot them, their pilots unable to adjust to Casey's unexpected maneuver.

"Gamnilians are so stupid," Casey said.

I opened my mouth to agree, but stopped short when I saw another fighter fly out of the hangar, speeding right for us. "Look," I said, pointing to the screen.

"Got it."

I checked our shields: 66%. "Hey, our shields must've regenerated."

"Perfect." She adjusted course so that we faced them head-on. Her thumb hovered over the black button. "Give me a target."

I tapped the button and touched the screen, but the box was way bigger than the ship at this distance. I couldn't center it. "Just a sec." Every time I adjusted the box, the Gamnilian spaceship seemed to squirm just outside the tiny sweet spot in the middle.

They sent the first volley, missing, but not by much. Casey responded by pressing the black button and holding it down. "Aaaaaaaaaaah!" she cried, our fighter locked in a guns-blazing game of chicken with our foe.

Lots of misses, both sides. A few hits. SHIELDS AT 57%. The fighters' weapons seemed to do more damage than the soldiers'.

"Casey!" I showed her the computer. "The shields."

She swung the spacecraft hard to port, and the engines howled, straining to obey their almost impossible orders. The other ship whizzed past. We were close to the Deathfighter now, and arced past it just in time to see a couple more fighters shoot out of the hangar to join the party.

My ring buzzed just as two more shots flew past, this time from behind.

Casey, still working the controls, wriggled up onto her knees and nodded at the tablet. "Put it against the wall," she said, her eyes glued to the display as she darted here and there, evading our enemy.

I leaned it up for her and she settled in, kneeling at an angle to the wall, her legs tucked underneath her.

I sat on the floor beside her, legs crossed. The ring still vibrated on my finger. I knew it was the map, but I didn't know how to get it. I lifted my fist. "Hello?"

A recorded male voice responded. "Incoming data. To view, say, 'Yes.' To store the file for later, say, 'Save.' In order to refuse the transmission, say—"

"Yes!" Casey shook her head, but but remained focused on the controller.

A greenish holographic map popped up above my ring. The image, almost the size of the tablet I'd been using, lay parallel to my fingers, so I unclenched and lowered my hand to get a better look. The diagram pivoted as I moved so that the front of the Deathfighter remained at the top of the map, farthest away from me. A red dot pulsed in the top left corner.

"Okay," I told Casey. "I've got it."

"Good," she answered. "Which way?"

I looked down to see several orange streaks zip past our fighter from two different directions, and the shields at 43%. She obviously hadn't been able to dodge them all. The camera showed the starboard side of the massive vessel, midship, seconds away. "Your target's on the far side. On top, near the front."

"Perfect," she replied. Another shot slammed into us. Casey held steady. Just when I thought she'd either lost control of the ship or her mind, she made her move and the little spacecraft dropped, slipping just centimetres beneath the belly of the beast.

"Show me," she said.

I turned my hand and the map spun around.

"K." She nodded, then with her free hand, pointed to an area near the middle. "So we're here, right?"

"Yeah. Looks about right."

She studied the layout. "Okay, so if we—"

"Casey!" I pointed to the computer. We'd just come out from under the Deathfighter, and a Gamnilian fighter swooped down on us from above, firing. Two blasts, two direct hits.

Casey threw the ship left, then down, then flipped it right over and back along the bottom of the Deathfighter, upside down. Just watching it made me nauseous. "Glad we're not actually in there," I said.

A long, slow smile stretched across Casey's lips. "But," she said, "they are." The fighter hugged the front of the Deathfighter as it shot out from under it. It sped up past the hangar door, narrowly missing another spaceship that popped out of the hole we'd made earlier, sending their craft shooting off at an awkward angle.

"Incoming! Three o'clock!"

She flipped the ship straight back, away from the Deathfighter, and the enemy followed its wasted shots off into space, unable to correct in time.

Casey explained her strategy. "They can't handle the G's." She looped back around toward our objective, and was immediately pursued by yet another Gamnilian. She adjusted her course, speeding for the front of the Deathfighter, but serpentine, rocking and rolling from side to side. At the last possible second, she cranked it hard to starboard, once again just avoiding impact, her enemy forced to peel off. "*And* they don't wanna die. Advantage, us."

It seemed to be working. "Great. Just get us there."

"Is there a certain spot we need to hit? To knock out a force field or something?"

I looked back at the map. Just a red light flashing in one corner. "I dunno." Even raising my hand closer to my face, it was hard to see much detail, and the writing appeared to be Gamnilian. "Can't tell."

"See if you can zoom in." She flipped the fighter around a few more times, dodging enemy ships and most of their fiery weapons. Yellow letters flashed at the top of the screen: SHIELDS AT 19%. "I don't wanna do all this for nothing."

I leaned in close. "Zoom," I said. Nothing. "Expand image." Same result. I reached out a finger. As soon as it met the hologram, the map shimmered. I poked at one of the rooms, and another image appeared above it—a photograph, taken from near the ceiling, showing the room's interior.

Touching that, I discovered a couple things. First, I was able to move it, not only side to side, but also vertically, so that it stood up, facing me. Then, I found that if I touched it with several fingers and spread them apart, I could expand it.

"You find anything?" Casey's thumbs danced, and the camera showed a dizzying array of zigs and zags. "I'm almost there. I need you to guide me in. We've only got one shot at this."

"Right." I swept the image off to one side.

"At the front, right?" she asked. "Port side?"

"Yup." I reached for the part of the map with the dot and spread my fingers, expanding it. It zoomed in. "Okay. The target's in the corner of the room." Realizing that wouldn't help Casey much, I looked for a landmark. The Deathfighter widened where that room met the one beside it. "Aim for the spot just past the front of the ship where the hull bends out."

"Come at it from the side or the top?"

I glanced up to see an orange blur streak across the window. "Side." *But how high?*

"Good." She swung the fighter around. Two more ships, half a dozen more bursts; two more hits before Casey broke free.

SHIELDS at 5%.

Yikes. I poked at the red dot, hoping a picture might show me our target and give me something I could pass on to Casey. The photo popped up, and I set it up in front of me, expanding it.

"Am I good?" she called over the whine of the fighter's engines.

It was hard to tell. The video looked like it was being shot from a roller coaster. She was going all serpentine again, but vertically: up, down, up down. I glanced to the left. The front of the Deathfighter was too far away. "No!" I pointed at a spot on the screen. "Over there."

She veered to port, dipped, then soared up through a barrage of enemy fire and into a back loop that brought her around farther back than we'd been before, but almost in line with our target.

"Nice! You see it?" I indicated an area just before the hull widened.

"Got it." As the Gamnilian fighters repositioned themselves, she began a series of erratic movements designed to keep our enemies from targeting us, all the while zeroing in on our objective. Several shots flew past the camera from different directions before one made contact with a thud. The computer let out a shrill beep, and three words appeared on the screen in flashing red letters. ALERT: SHIELD FAILURE.

I turned my attention back to the picture that floated in front of me, which had been taken from up high in one corner of a big room. If our target was in that corner, it was right below the camera and I couldn't see it. I scanned the room. Two of the corners were visible. Nothing to see. The view of the third was blocked.

"Here we go, baby!" Casey levelled out, and moving in a straight line now, the fighter accelerated. A few seconds and we—

Something about the room . . .

Casey held down the red button, sending glowing plasma hurtling ahead of the craft, slamming into the battleship's hull, one explosion after another.

I couldn't see the last corner. Crates. Barrels. *No!* "Wait! Stop! That's where Geet—"

A flash lit up the room. Then the camera went dark.

27 Together

"What?" Casey knelt right next to me, but her confused voice might as well have been miles away.

I stared at the computer. It stared back, its blank screen almost a reflection. Just two words: CONNECTION LOST.

"Simon, what?" She lowered the controller to her lap.

I raised my eyes, found hers. "Geet . . ." I swallowed. "That . . . was his hideout."

"What?" She looked at the picture, still hovering where I'd left it, less than an arm's length in front of my face. "What do you mean?" She raised herself to one knee and edged closer to get a better look.

I pointed at the photo, my finger over the hidden corner of the room. "See? That's it. Where we hit."

She studied the image. "That could be any storage room."

"Look at the barrels. And the crates," I said, my finger indicating each.

She shrugged. "I'm sure they have those in all their storerooms."

"All stacked in one corner?" I ran my finger along a deep metal shelf that stretched along one wall, from above the storage containers to the far end of the room. "Remember this?" Geet had said there was a second level. "Where he put the Doctor?"

She stared at the picture for a moment before speaking. "He got out," she said with a nod. "No way he was still in there when we hit it."

"How do you know?" I really wanted her to convince me.

She rose and took a few steps across the room before turning back toward me. "He knew we were coming! Geet's not stupid."

"Of course not." I twisted toward her, placing one hand on the floor for support, the other on my raised knee. "But he said what he was doing was important, and that he wouldn't leave 'til it was done."

"Yeah, important. But worth dying for?"

As I pushed myself up from the floor, I noticed that the holographic map still glowed just beyond the red circle of light on my ring. I lifted my hand to my mouth. "What am I supposed to say? Off? No . . . Save file." The ring went dark. I returned my attention to my sister. "Remember when Geet said that we couldn't ever let Lusec find Dad's machine?"

"Yeah . . ."

"Remember why?"

"He'd use it to take over the galaxy."

"Right. I'm guessing that's the same reason he didn't want Lusec to get his teleporter."

"Makes sense. That's why he got us to blow it up." She shrugged. "But he finished that. He was just deleting some files."

"So Lusec wouldn't get them." I stepped toward her. "It wasn't just the teleporter. He said there was other stuff too. He was willing to stay behind to keep it from the Gamnilians, even if it meant being captured again. If whatever was in those files was dangerous, don't you think Geet would risk his life to save the galaxy?"

Casey took a breath, let it out slowly, then brought up something else neither of us wanted to deal with. "He said we needed to go to the shuttle as soon as we crashed the fighter."

"*You* said we weren't leaving without him."

"I know." She gave a helpless shrug. "But . . . we have to. Right now we don't know where he is, or even if he's . . ." She looked down for just a moment. When she raised her head again, the fire was back in her eyes. "What are we gonna do? Wait here until the Gamnilians figure out we're alive and come looking for us? This is our chance."

"He's the only reason we *have* a chance! We can't just leave him."

"Simon, this is Geet we're talking about. If he's alive, he knows where we're going. He'll find a way to get there."

"What if he's not?"

"Then I'm not gonna hang around here and throw away what he did for us." She turned and strode to the door, her hand perched on the lever that served as a handle.

"What if—"

"What if, what if. That's your problem, Simon. Sometimes it's better not to think too much." She pulled the handle and the door inched open, revealing the darkness beyond it. "Sometimes you gotta think, and sometimes you just gotta *do.*"

"Sure, but we can't just go running off without Geet."

Casey swung the door wide open as if she was about to go through, then stopped. She studied my face for a moment, then said, "You sure this is about Geet?"

She might as well have slapped me across the face. "What?"

Letting go of the handle, she took a step toward me. "He said the hangar's just through the door at the other end of this hallway, right?" She pointed into the darkness.

"Yeah . . ."

"We open that door and everything gets real. Gamnilians, blasters—real ones, that can kill us. We've done some pretty scary stuff since we left home, but whatever's on the other side of that door is probably gonna be even scarier. And we don't have Geet to help us. But it's the only way home."

For a moment the only sound was the humming of the machine at the end of the room. I looked down at the floor, hard and black, and something Geet had said popped into my mind. "Sometimes the path to safety leads through danger."

"Uh huh."

I looked up at my sister.

Her bloodshot eyes were a reminder of everything we'd been through. "Remember what we said? The only way we're gonna make it is together."

I nodded.

"Well, here we are—you and me. I got your back, Simon."

"Yeah." I nodded again. "Me too." I smiled. "And your front."

We shared a brief chuckle, then stepped through the door. Together.

28 Distractions

Casey raced out into the hangar, crossing the two-metre gap from the doorway to the back of a boxy-looking ship parked there. Spinning to flatten her back against the rear of the spacecraft, she gestured for me to follow.

My stomach flipped. I stepped forward, just short of the doorway, took a breath, then leaned forward to peer out. All clear to the right. To the left, a dozen or so small to medium-sized spaceships sat parked in a long line, all with their backs to us. The third one down was the *Valiant*. No Gamnilians.

Sometimes you just gotta do. I did, launching myself into the open. For the first time, I was grateful for the Gamnilians' obsession with dim lighting.

I mistimed my turn, my backside and shoulders bumping up against the back of the vessel to Casey's left. Beside me, Casey raised a finger to her lips, an unnecessary reminder to be quiet.

Most of the massive airdock lay in the same direction as the *Valiant*, stretching for well over a hundred metres to our right. I saw no Gamnilians, but heard deep, muffled voices along with other noises that suggested activity down near that end of the room. There seemed to be others talking somewhere else as well. The metal walls and huge space played tricks with the sound, so it was difficult to tell. I guessed that they were at the other end, but farther over—in the middle, or on the far side.

Casey shuffled along the back of the ship, which was almost twice as big as ours, then poked her head around the corner. After a few seconds, she looked back at me and flashed a thumbs up. Then she pointed to her right, toward the *Valiant*.

I nodded, took a step.

A flash. Electricity crackled and Gamnilian voices began to shout.

We stopped cold, heads swinging side to side trying to figure out what was happening and where. The two groups of Gamnilians seemed to be yelling across the hangar.

Casey pointed to herself, then with two fingers, to her eyes and back around the corner. Then she gestured for me to take a look around my side.

As soon as I turned back the other way, I caught sight of movement on the wall ahead of us. A little less than halfway to the end of the room on our left, a large square vent sat about a metre off the floor. The grate had just disappeared into the opening.

I reached over and tapped Casey's arm. She turned and watched along with me as two little hands emerged, gripping the sides of the opening, followed by a brown mop of hair. Two huge, dark eyes gazed in our direction, and even from there I could see them sparkle. *Geet!*

I sprung forward, but Casey grabbed my arm and pulled me back. "There's no cover!" she hissed.

She was right. The only spaceship past our hiding spot was a large one, farther out from the wall. It sat up high, and I could easily be seen if I stepped out. But so could Geet, who hurried to cover his tracks, replacing the grate.

I slid across the back of the ship, then peered around the edge. The hangar was wider than I remembered. Sixty or seventy metres away, a huge black warship stood in the middle of the enormous room, reminding me of a gigantic, deadly spider.

Beneath it I was able to make out more spacecraft parked along the far wall, along with the source of the zapping and hollering. Sparks poured from a control panel near the back corner. Two soldiers looked on, apparently arguing about what to do about it. From time to time, one or both would turn to bellow across the hangar at the other group.

I turned to see Geet racing toward us, his tiny feet making no sound. He wore the utility belt I'd filled for him, along with a black backpack. In no time he arrived, hugging each of us in turn, then slipping into the empty space between us. He held the square device I'd placed in one of the pouches of his belt, confirming my suspicion. I jerked my thumb back in the direction of the sparkfest. "You?"

He nodded, grinning. "I can make distractions too," he whispered.

Casey smiled for just a moment before her serious face returned. She nodded toward our shuttle.

Geet shook his head, holding up a hand. Bare Gamnilian feet slapped the floor, moving away from the front of the room and toward the sparking control panel. After a few seconds, apparently satisfied that the coast was clear, he lowered his arm and nodded.

Casey led the way, then Geet. I followed after them, copying their light, hunched-over run, so that we were like three mice scurrying after a bit of cheese. Dashing between ships, I swung my head to the right to catch another glimpse of the commotion on the other side. Two more Gamnilians, wearing the same grey uniforms as the ones in the other hangar, were just arriving on the scene.

As I passed behind the next spacecraft, I paid the price for looking the other way. My foot slammed into a black

196

cylindrical object less than a metre high, knocking it over and sending it skittering under the craft.

I sprawled to the floor, toes burning. Flipping onto my back I raised my head, seeing Casey and Geet frozen mid-stride, staring wide-eyed at the back of the ship.

The rear hatch was open, revealing that the cylinder was attached by cable to a heavy box-shaped device that sat at the back of the cargo area. Two heavy wrench-like instruments had been left atop it, and when the cylinder reached the end of its tether, the box tipped, sending the tools over the edge. Geet, who was nearest, shot out an arm to catch them, but they fell end over end past his outstretched hand, landing with a clatter on the black metal floor. The bulky box brought up the rear, punctuating the disaster with a thump that resounded throughout the hangar.

A new round of shouting arose, followed by the sound of Gamnilian feet running in our direction. Geet pointed at the *Valiant*. "Go! Go!"

Casey reached the door in a flash, fumbling briefly with the latch, then swinging it open. I pushed myself to my feet and began to make my way to the door when I noticed Geet, head bowed over the device in his hands. He tapped the screen, and across the hangar—the front corner this time—a loud buzzer sounded.

More hollering. I listened for clues, sifting through the racket that now seemed to be competing against itself—the chaos of crackling electricity versus the rhythmic pulsing of the alarm. The Gamnilian footfalls stopped briefly, then started up again. Different directions. They'd split up. Which meant that one was still coming our way.

I turned back toward the shuttle and jogged the last steps to the door. One hand on the opening, ready to pull myself in, I glanced back, expecting to see Geet right behind me. Instead, I caught a glimpse of his blue suit as he disappeared behind the next craft. "Geet?"

Casey, who'd been muttering to herself up front, called back, "What're you doing? Get in!"

At that moment, Geet's head popped into view above the ship next to ours. It took me a second to make sense of it—he was on *top* of the cargo ship where we'd first hidden, his back to me, dancing and waving like a little kid who wanted his mommy to see him on stage at the Christmas concert. Then the muffled explosion of a Gamnilian blaster, and he dropped out of sight.

No! A cold wave of shock flooded my body. I turned and stumbled to the end of the next spacecraft, where I peeked around the corner, knees shaking.

An orange blast streaked across my view and slammed into the wall just as a little blue-clothed alien shot out from between the two vessels and tore around the back of the farther one. Relief. *Geet does it again.*

I slipped out of sight as soon as his pursuer emerged, lumbering after him. Geet was buying us time. But how long could he keep this up? I glanced at our little shuttle. No engine sounds.

Another explosion was immediately followed by yet another on the far side of the room. More angry yelling back and forth. I snuck nearer to the front of the ship I was hiding behind and peered past it. Smoke rose from a Gamnilian spacecraft—the one closest to the sparking panel. The soldier chasing Geet had missed his target, hitting one of his own ships, and the guys in grey were really letting him have it.

The sound of feet rapidly pounding the floor pulled me back to my spot at the rear of the ship. They stopped for a moment, then started again. I strained to hear, but all the noise around me made it impossible. I risked another peek just as Geet darted around the end of the spaceship again, followed seconds later by the enraged soldier. He had the Gamnilian running around the ship like a big old dog chasing a squirrel around a tree.

I looked back at the *Valiant*. Still no engines. *Come on, Casey!* The back of the craft looked like the surface of the moon, the goop from the fire extinguisher having hardened, forming a grey crust over the scorched paint and metal. I wondered whether Casey was wasting her time trying to start the engines, and what we'd do if she didn't succeed.

Geet flew by again, skidding a little as he rounded the back of the ship, once again disappearing behind it. I waited for the soldier. Heard him running. But he didn't show. More footfalls, but which direction? Then a rifle blast, and Geet diving onto his stomach and sliding out past the far end of the cargo ship. The shot streaked above his body and blew apart one of the machines near the wall.

Geet had been moving fast, and try as he might, could not stop the slide that carried him right into the smoldering pile of rubble. As the huge Gamnilian bore down on him, he leapt to his feet and dodged off to one side. But another large piece of equipment blocked his path, and bumping into it, he fell to the floor. The gigantic soldier was right there with his rifle pointed directly at him.

Geet was cornered.

29 Now or Never

The Gamnilian towered over him. "Where you run now, little *bahkh?*" he rumbled.

Our small friend just cowered at his feet.

The soldier, who stood at an angle to Geet, stared down the barrel of his blaster. *"Pahkht!"* he shouted, and his terrified prisoner jumped. Laughing, he lowered the weapon a little and tapped his belt. After a few seconds, he began speaking Gamnilian to whoever had answered his call. As they talked—the soldier alternating between speaking and pausing to listen to a voice we couldn't hear—Geet's eyes darted to and fro between his captor and his surroundings.

For a moment, our gaze met. He gave a tiny shake of his head, looked up at the Gamnilian, then back at me. Nodding toward the *Valiant*, his eyes begged me to go.

"*T'k dja'tang. K'dekh.*" The soldier tapped his belt again, then looked down at his prisoner. "They say I not shoot. Commodore want you." Stepping forward, he bent over and grabbed Geet's arm, his enormous hand swallowing Geet's entire bicep. He jerked him to his feet like a child might lift a rag doll. "Go!" he said, jabbing his gun toward the exit at the end of the room.

As Geet turned to march off to his appointment with the commodore, someone yelled from over by the sparking panel.

"Stop," the Gamnilian commanded his captive, before calling back across the hangar.

Desperate to free Geet, my eyes ransacked the area around me, finally falling upon a bulky green tank attached to the wall. A fat, grey hose hung down from it. There was some Gamnilian writing on the tank, as well as a symbol: flames. I glanced at the back of our ship, remembering the disgusting liquid that had dripped from it after the fire.

Geet's guy now had his back fully turned as he shouted back and forth with his comrades. This was my chance.

The fire extinguisher hung near the door we'd come through when we entered, about halfway to my target. I'd have to make a run for it. Remembering Geet running silently across the floor earlier, I ripped off my boots.

My heart thumped against my chest. One. Two. Three! I dashed for my weapon, sliding my feet along the smooth floor with each step—hop-slide, hop-slide—eyes on the Gamnilian all the way.

I skidded to a stop just as a whoop arose from the far side of the hangar. I listened. No more sparking. If those two weren't busy at the panel over there, they'd soon be on their way over here.

It was now or never. Reaching up and grasping the tank with both hands, I wrestled the heavy thing down and into my arms, hugging it tightly against my body. I didn't see a lever to turn it on. But there was a metal collar at the end of the hose that might—

The *Valiant's* engines sprung to life behind me. The Gamnilian stopped mid-sentence and whirled around. I reached for the end of the hose, felt the tank slipping, shifted my weight. As I struggled to regain my balance, the soldier raised his gun. I let myself drop to the floor, feeling the heat as the blast whizzed above me.

The tank clanked to the floor beside me, its hose falling across my belly. As the Gamnilian took aim a second time, I grabbed the hose with both hands and twisted the collar.

Foosh! A powerful burst of greenish-grey goo geysered toward its target in an arc that was both disgusting and beautiful. The alien's eyes and mouth were wide open with shock as the slushy liquid slopped over his face. He raised both hands to his eyes and staggered back several steps, gagging and spitting.

Geet was free! Grabbing the soldier's rifle, he raced for the *Valiant*.

The enraged guard swept some of the goo from his eyes, then charged with a roar. I pushed myself up onto one knee, glanced at the open door of our shuttle, then back at him. One more shot, just to be safe. *Foooooosh!* I held it as long as I dared, then dropped the hose and made a run for it.

I tumbled into the *Valiant* after Geet, who hurried to the front, stashed the blaster in a cubby and jumped up into a half crouch on the seat beside Casey.

"Close the door!" Casey barked, busy at the controls.

Scrambling to my feet, I reached outside the ship and grabbed the handle as the enraged Gamnilian, covered in sludge, attempted to run after us. My last shot had been rushed and much of the goop had hit the floor. One big, bare foot skidded, and in spite of flailing madly in a useless attempt to regain his balance, he landed on his back with a *whump!* As I hauled on the door, the soldier pushed himself him to his feet and made a last, desperate lunge. His feet slipped out from under him and he splashed face-first in a pool of slop just as the door slammed shut.

Running forward, I heard Geet say, "Computer, activate copilot control console." Just in front of him, a rectangular section of the dashboard lifted, while another narrower part slid forward—a computer monitor and control pad.

That would've been good to know.

"Simon, you sit here."

As we switched places, Casey called out, "The other one's coming!" The soldier who'd been dealing with the alarm at the front now sprinted toward us, weapon raised.

"Computer, deploy shields," I said.

A blast leapt from his gun. The spacecraft shuddered, orange light flashing across the window, deflected by the force field.

Casey looked up and nodded her approval. "Good job."

"Forward shields at 95%," the computer told us.

Geet, standing beside me, took a tiny remote control from his belt and aimed it at the gigantic black door that blocked our exit. "More soldiers will come soon. We must go!"

The onrushing Gamnilian swung his shocked face toward the slowly rising door and skidded to a halt. The exit's force field was the only thing keeping him from being sucked out into space. He fired off another shot at us that missed its target, then pivoted to race back to the control station in the corner where he'd been trying, unsuccessfully, to stop the buzzing alarm.

Our little vessel popped up from the floor. Casey bit her lip, nudged the joystick forward, and the *Valiant* eased ahead. As we emerged from behind the shuttle to our right, we were hit with a series of blasts. The grey-suited Gamnilians had taken cover behind the landing gear of the large spaceship near the end of the hangar. Now they unleashed a barrage from their sidearms.

Casey jerked us to a stop, snapping my head forward, then slid back, taking a couple more hits before fully returning to cover.

"Starboard shields at 76%."

"Go!" I cried.

Casey shook her head. "Remember how the Gamnilians were chasing us before they pulled us in?"

I finished her thought for her. "Our rear shields are out."

She knew that to get out of the door, we'd have to expose the back of the ship. "The reactor almost blew once. If we take another hit back there . . ."

Boom.

"We cannot stay here." Geet reached over to input some commands on my computer. In a moment, the screen displayed a wide-angle view of the wall behind us. "Rear cameras," he explained. "We will back out."

Casey's face scrunched up with confusion. "What?"

He pointed at the exit. "Out of the hangar. To protect our reactor."

"That's cra—"

Two more blasts thumped into us. The two Gamnilians who'd hit us before had moved, and were now hiding behind the front of the craft to our right, firing away.

"Go!" Geet said.

Casey shoved the joystick ahead and to the right—away from the exit—and our little cargo shuttle shot forward,

206

missing the front of next ship by centimetres and sending the Gamnilians diving for safety. Then we veered left to avoid crashing into the vessel they'd hid behind earlier.

As soon as we passed it, I spotted a bigger problem. "They're coming!" I shouted as I struggled to pull on my seat belt. The double doors at the end of the shuttle bay were wide open, and a dozen Gamnilian soldiers poured through.

At the sight of us, they raised their blasters. Casey hesitated only briefly before swerving right at them, sending them scrambling for cover, firing off bursts as they ran. At the last second, Casey yanked the joystick left, and the little spaceship groaned as it executed a turn it was not designed to make.

After wiping out a table, some shelving and various pieces of equipment along the wall, we looped around to the left. We were headed right for two little fighters just like the one we'd hijacked in the other airdock. Casey pulled back on a handle to her left and the nose lifted, allowing us to sneak up and over them, along with some larger ships parked along the wall beyond them.

"Starboard shields at 54%. Forward shields—"

"Computer, merge shields," Geet called from somewhere behind us, having been flung into the wall and onto the floor. I turned to see him flip down the bottom of one of the two jump seats along the wall behind Casey, and strap himself in.

"Confirmed," the electronic voice replied. "Rear shields remain offline. Remaining shields merged at 72%."

As the Gamnilians recovered, shots began to slam into our port side. We continued our hard arc to the left, swinging out into the middle of the hangar. From there, Casey dropped us right down until, with a screeching of metal, we contacted the floor and skidded to a stop not two metres away from a spacecraft just four ships down from our original parking spot.

"What are you doing?" I asked Casey as blaster fire blazed all around us, several shots whacking into our rapidly failing shields.

Casey didn't wait around to answer. She popped us up off the floor, then backed up. The pitch of the engines increased, and from behind us came the familiar rhythmic beeping made by reversing cargo vehicles everywhere.

"Simon," she called, steering in a jittery path toward the exit. "Guide me!"

The backup camera showed the ships on the far side quickly getting closer. "Slow down!" I called.

We jerked to a stop. I was going to have whiplash.

"Sorry! Backwards is touchy." She pulled ahead, stopped, then reversed again, only slightly slower than last time. *Beep, beep, beep.*

The Gamnilians raced toward us, weapons firing.

My gaze returned to the monitor. She was too far to the left. We'd miss the door and hit the front wall. "Right!"

"I'm going right!"

"More right!"

"That's as far as—"

"Stop!"

We halted just a hair away from the wall. Less than 20 metres to our left stood the soldier at his workstation, struggling to regain control of the force field. Casey waved as he glanced in our direction, and he replied by firing off a shot with one hand that slammed into our port side.

"Shields at 36%."

We shot forward, the *Valiant* running along the line of vessels to our left. Then we slowed, coming to a stop under an onslaught of blaster fire.

"We can't keep taking these hits!" I said, as more blasts flew at us from the front. Most of the Gamnilians had taken cover behind the landing gear of the black spider-ship, while others sprinted for the ships along the side of the hangar, joining their comrades who'd already begun firing from there.

Geet's little voice rose up from behind us. "I have an idea. Go!"

As Casey pulled back on the joystick, I looked over my shoulder to see him press a button on his remote. The Gamnilians shot forward several meters, rifles ripped from their hands. Another press of the button followed the first almost immediately, and they sprawled on the floor.

I laughed, looking back at Geet. "How'd you do that?"

"The force field," he replied simply, with a tiny smile.

It took me a moment to figure it out. He'd turned off the force field just long enough that they were all sucked toward the door, then turned it back on again.

The beeping of the back-up alarm pulled my attention back to the camera. Casey had swung it too far around. "Left!"

The back of the spacecraft turned to port at the exact same moment the starboard camera winked out. Speeding backward with half the screen blank, I couldn't tell whether we'd make it. "Whoa!"

We jerked to a stop.

"Geet!" Casey called. Several of the Gamnilians had managed to recover their guns and were taking aim. Beyond them a dozen or more reinforcements stormed into the hangar.

He pushed the button again.

We roared forward just as the Gamnilians lurched toward the door, one sailing right at us before dropping in a heap on the floor with the others. We flew right over him and two others as Casey lined us up as best she could with the door, stopping pretty much in the middle of the massive space.

"Here goes."

We shot back, engines wailing, beeper beeping. The second camera came online again, and we saw that this time we were headed right for the middle of the opening. The stars beyond seemed to beckon us out to freedom.

At the last moment, the bald back of a Gamnilian head rose into view. It spun, jaw dropping, then threw itself back down, narrowly escaping death as we once again soared over him.

210

Geet hit the button, we shot through the gap, and he hit it again. Looking through the front window now, I watched the Gamnilian soldiers surge forward like a rag doll army, then drop as one. Almost. The poor guy we'd run over (twice) was too close to the door. He flew face-first into the shield like a bug into a window. Arms and legs splayed, he slid slowly down until he settled in a trembling pile on the floor. He was gonna need some time in sick bay.

30 Valiant

Geet sat in the copilot's seat, setting a course for his home planet while Casey looked on. He kept his head down as he entered data into the computer, never once looking out the window. He really didn't like flying.

When we first escaped the Deathfighter, Casey had turned the *Valiant* around and kicked it up to *Maximum Light*. After just a few minutes, he'd suggested that we slow down to input our flight plan.

"What about the Gamnilians?" Casey asked. "Won't they follow us?"

Sitting beside me in the copilot's seat, Geet shook his head.

"What?" she said. "Why not?"

"When you were flying the fighter, I was busy too." Here he allowed himself a little smile. "I . . . did something to their engines."

I laughed. "What did you do?"

"Well, when they try to go to light speed . . ." He turned up his palms and shrugged. "Nothing."

"You shut down their engines?"

He giggled.

"Wait a minute," Casey said. "What about all those other ships they have? In the shuttle bay. And the fighters. Couldn't they catch us with those?"

"They could," Geet answered calmly, "if they could get them out of the hangar." Seeing our puzzled faces, he continued. "Nothing can leave the Deathfighter if its shields are on."

"Oh yeah." I smiled, remembering the last Gamnilian we saw as we flew away. "The shield across the door."

"Yes . . . but they will fix that soon. And there are fighters in the other hangar also," he said. "So I turned on their *outer* shields."

"The big ones?" Casey asked.

Geet nodded.

"Won't they just turn them off?"

"They will try."

"Geet," she said, "you're the best."

*   *   *

With the course laid in, all that was left for Casey to do was crank the speed back up. From there, the shuttle would fly itself.

Geet retreated to a back corner of the cabin and sat on the floor with his arms wrapped around his legs, which were tucked up to his chest. I joined him, leaning back against the wall near the door, forearms resting on my raised knees.

"So," Casey turned and knelt on her seat so that she looked at him over her headrest, "how long will it take to get to your planet at this speed?"

"About two hours," Geet answered.

"What about the Gamnilians?" I asked. "They won't just be sitting around having a tea party. Will they be able to fix their engines?"

Geet nodded.

Casey rose from her chair. "How long?"

"I think . . . maybe one hour."

As she walked around behind her seat, I asked, "Then how long will it take them to get to your planet?"

"Probably . . . one hour."

She joined us on the floor. "So . . ."

Geet shifted uncomfortably. "It might be . . . close."

214

It was quiet for a moment until Casey noticed my feet. "Hey, where are your shoes?"

"Well . . . that's kind of a long story."

"It sounds like we have time."

I told her how Geet had risked his life so we could escape.

"Wow," she replied. "I mean, no offense or anything Geet, but . . . well, you just always seemed kind of afraid to me."

He took a moment before responding. "Brave is not . . . how you *feel*. It is . . . what you *do*." He turned to me. "Simon, how did you feel when the Gamnilian aimed his rifle at you?"

"Uh . . . pretty scared," I understated.

"But you shot him with the hose. You . . ." He blinked, his big eyes glistening. "You saved me."

"Wait," Casey said. "What?"

I explained about Geet's capture, and how I took off my boots to make a run for the fire extinguisher. As I told the story, it felt like I was talking about someone else.

"He had a blaster?"

"Aimed right at me."

"You shot a Gamnilian with a fire hose?"

I shrugged.

"Really?" Casey looked at me almost as if we'd never met before. "Wow."

It was hard for me to believe too.

She was eager to hear more of the story, so we filled her in on some of the details. Then she told us a little about what went on inside the shuttle, and why it took so long to start the engines. Apparently the fire had caused some damage that forced her to try out some things that weren't in the manual.

When story time was over, she turned her eyes toward Geet. "So, any shopping malls around here?"

He just looked confused.

"We need to buy Simon a new pair of boots. If we run around outside the house without our shoes on, our mom gets really mad. Says it's dangerous."

"Hey," I laughed. "She's right. I almost got shot!"

Casey returned to the pilot's chair and sat down. "Go little ship, go," she said. "Hey, spaceships have names, don't they? What's this one called?"

"The *Valiant*," I answered.

"*Valiant*." Geet repeated. "Brave." He smiled. "I think that is a very good name."

*   *   *

The streaking stars became sparkling points of light as the autopilot dropped us out of lightspeed. We'd entered the Celidian System, and were now only ten minutes from Geet's home—as long as we got there before the Gamnilians.

Geet had been working away at the copilot control console, but now he tapped the touchscreen controls one last time and leaned back. "There."

Casey had been watching from her chair, but I'd just wandered forward from my spot on the floor. "What did you just do?" I asked from where I stood, each hand resting on a seat back.

He turned in his chair and folded his legs. "Our rear shields are working now. And I boosted our other ones."

"Hopefully we won't need them," I said. I couldn't shake the feeling that the Gamnilians would show up any second.

"I do not think we will. They have not shown up on our scans."

"You don't think they're coming?"

"They will come. But we should be able to get to my home first. That is very good."

"I guess it took 'em longer than you thought it would to fix their ship." Casey grinned. "Where'd you learn to do all this stuff, anyway?"

A faraway look slipped across Geet's face, and he lowered his head. When he finally spoke, he stared at the console in front of him. "When I was a child—very small— the Gamnilians . . . destroyed my home. I was saved, but I . . . never saw my parents again."

He got up and began to walk back to the cargo area. "Once I was old enough to understand, I made up my mind to fight. To stop them." He turned, his tiny fists clenched at his side. "Children should not be taken from their families."

"So," Casey looked confused, "you're a soldier? Who do you fight with?"

"Oh no." He shook his head. "I do not fight like that. I work with others who stand against the Gamnilians— Casimonians, Celidians, the Havek'dal. To make technology that will stop them. I do not kill."

"What about the Doctor?" I wandered over to the wall behind the copilot's seat and leaned against it. "When we blew up your hideout."

"Do not worry. I teleported him out before I left."

"Where'd you put him?"

"In the sewage recycling facility."

"Gross!" Casey and I both exclaimed.

He shrugged. "Not for him. That is what Bombulans eat."

"That explains a lot," Casey said.

There was one more thing. "And what about the Gamnilians in the other hangar—with the fighters? Wouldn't they have been sucked out into space when we made the hole in the door?"

Casey opened two new windows on her computer. "I didn't see any when we flew out."

"I do not think so," Geet answered. "Both hangars have another set of shields they can turn on, and a different control panel at the back."

The computer beeped several times and the *Valiant* shifted. "Impact averted."

Casey scanned the readouts on her monitor. "What was that?"

"Probably a meteoroid," Geet replied.

I sat down beside Casey in the copilot's seat. "I didn't see anything."

"Computer, access forward cameras," Geet said. "Replay last 15 seconds." The video appeared on our screens as he moved to stand beside my chair. It showed exactly what I'd seen earlier through the window.

"There," he said, reaching forward to point at the screen. "Magnify quadrant four and restart." The camera zoomed in. "Freeze." He leaned forward and with a finger, drew a circle in the air above a tiny grey dot. "See? Computer, isolate nearest object. Maximum magnification."

The meteoroid filled the screen.

"It looks like a rock," I said.

"That's a meteor?" Casey asked. "Where's the fire?"

Geet smiled. "They only burn up when they enter a planet's atmosphere."

"How big is it?" she asked.

He shrugged. "Maybe . . . as big as your fist."

"So, pretty small."

He turned to go back and sit down away from the window. "Big enough to destroy a spacecraft much larger than this one."

"Whoa."

I leaned forward to study the image. It actually looked like a fist: roundish on one side, four bumps on the other, and a pointy lump at one end. I was glad it hadn't gotten a chance to punch us.

"Arrival at destination in 6 minutes," droned the computer. "Autopilot will disengage in 60 seconds. Fasten safety restraints and prepare to pilot ship manually for landing." The joystick slowly dropped down from underneath the control panel.

Casey strapped herself in. As I reached for my seatbelts, I noticed that Geet remained beside me.

"I . . . need to guide Casey in," he explained when I looked up at him.

"Oh." I said. "Sure."

As he hopped into the copilot's chair beside Casey and buckled up, I wandered back to the cargo area. Flipping down the bottom of the jump seat closest to the front, I sat down.

"Autopilot will disengage in 30 seconds. Prepare to pilot ship manually for landing."

I reached back for the seat belts that hung from the wall behind me, struggling to untangle them. The *Valiant* slowed and its nose lifted as it set Casey up for the final approach.

"What's that?" Casey asked Geet.

I looked up at the large grey blob that had appeared ahead of us.

Geet clapped his hands. "My home!"

"*That's* where you live?"

"Yes. It is an asteroid."

"It looks like a potato," Casey said.

Geet didn't seem to notice her comment. "I live inside. If you—"

"Autopilot disengaged," interrupted the computer.

Casey maneuvered the joystick like a pro, so that we didn't even feel the transition. Eyes focused on our destination, she said, "Okay, Geet. What's the plan?"

"There is an entrance on the other side, about halfway up."

"Should I just fly underneath and loop back up?"

"Yes," he replied. "Once you enter the cave it will be . . . tricky. You must go very slowly. But the Gamnilians are not here yet—if they were chasing us, we would not make it." He began to explain what she'd need to do to get us safely through. Before long, things got ridiculously complicated— thrust mitigation, enhanced RPY dampeners, and something about the pros and cons of induction field navigation, I think.

I tried to keep up, but who was I kidding? I hadn't even been able to figure out my seat belts yet. There obviously wasn't a job for me, and I was tired of wrestling with the hopelessly tangled straps, so I just leaned back against the headrest and closed my eyes. It felt good. I was exhausted.

The little meteoroid drifted into my mind. I realized it was almost like a mini version of Geet's home. Maybe a piece of an asteroid broke off and had been hurtling through space all that time, farther and farther from its home, with no one even knowing it was there.

There was a lull in the conversation up front. "Hey, Geet," I called. "You said you had a plan to get us home. What—"

"Warning." The computer cut me off. "Alien vessel appro—"

The radio crackled to life. "Well, well, well." The voice was all too familiar. "It's the *children*. And their tiny friend in pyjamas."

I leapt to my feet and raced to stand behind the console to find that Lusec's sneering face had taken over both computer monitors. "Hide and seek is over, little ones. You lose."

31 On the Doorstep

A blast slammed into the back of the *Valiant*, throwing me to the floor. I clambered back onto my chair, scrambling for the safety restraints, just as we were hit again.

"Warning: Rear shields at 7%."

Looking between the front seats, I watched the commodore as he spoke once again, his face framed by shadows. "I have tried to be reasonable. I spared your lives and treated you as guests. But how was I repaid?" He leaned into the camera so that now our view extended only from the ugly scar above his left eye to just below his snarling lips. "With treachery! I do *not* like my ship damaged," he growled.

"I could crush you here and now. My battle officer awaits my command: One word from me, and your puny craft will be vapourized. Yet still I show mercy. You will receive a transmission outlining the necessary steps for the surrender of your vessel. Follow them precisely, and you will live. Once you are on board, I shall explain the one remaining option you have that does not result in your death." His face disappeared from the screen the second he stopped speaking.

We both looked at Geet, who bent over and began to dig through his backpack.

"What do we do?" I asked.

He pulled a tablet out of the bag. "I will tie this into the *Valiant's* computer. Once we receive their message, Simon, you can use this to tell Casey what she needs to do."

"What!" Casey exclaimed. "You're gonna do what he said?"

Geet set about syncing the device to the system. "For now, it is our only choice."

"What?" She pointed at the asteroid, which now towered over us. Soon, we'd pass beneath it. "We're almost there. Let's go!"

"They will follow. You cannot get through the cave quickly enough to escape them." He finished, then reached back between the seats with the tablet. "Start by lowering the shields. It will be on their list."

The computer beeped. "Message received from alien vessel."

I got up and took the tablet from Geet. "Where did they even come from?" I asked. "You said they didn't show up on our scans."

"I do not know. I have heard that the Gamnilians were working on a way to mask their ships' energy signatures, but I did not think . . ." His voice trailed off as several new files popped open on his computer.

"Well, we can't just do what he says," Casey said. "Do you seriously trust Lusec? If we drop the shields, he'll blow us to bits."

"I do not think so," Geet said without looking up. "He knows about your father's machine."

In the middle of opening the Gamnilian message, I froze. "What?"

"He is keeping us alive for a reason. He must have recovered the data from the brain probe."

"Then we definitely can't do what he says," Casey said. "This ship have any weapons?"

He looked up at her. "You are right. We cannot surrender. But we cannot fight. I am working on another plan—I have already accessed the main computer in my laboratory. But I need more time. You must make them believe we will cooperate." He returned his gaze to the monitor. "And . . . while you are doing it, learn everything you can about our weapons."

The Gamnilian message said we had five minutes to meet their demands. The eight items on their list included some obvious tasks, like lowering the shields, and some unexpected ones, like dimming the cabin lights. We went through each one, point by point. By the time the commodore's face reappeared on the monitors, we'd completed four of the first five, skipping the one that said to shut off the engines, which Geet said we should leave to the last possible moment.

"Your time is up," Lusec snapped.

"You wanna get that?" Casey said. "Kinda busy here."

Geet just stretched one hand back between the seats. "I need the tablet. I must finish!"

I stood and handed him the device. Casey had regained control of her monitor and continued to study a schematic of the *Valiant's* weaponry. They wanted *me* to do the talking? What was I supposed to say?

Lusec's face turned to one side. "Lieutenant Ka'tok, prepare to fire on my mark. Three . . . two . . ."

I lunged ahead, stabbing the rocker switch that flashed green on the console. "Stop!"

The skin on his bony eye ridges lifted and he brought his head back around. "The little commander has given us an order, Lieutenant Ka'tok. What do you think? Shall we obey?"

"Ba'neel't'nek d'at'na'tahk mot'k dawkh'k'tang f't'k mahg'tet tahn'nahg mot'k," his lieutenant replied off camera.

The commodore smiled. "Yet I am curious. Why do they delay? They *do* like games. Or is it more treachery?" Now his eyes narrowed. "Perhaps they have a death wish."

226

"No!" I blurted. "We're trying! We're almost done. We just have a few more left to finish."

"Including shutting off your engines. My engineer tells me you skipped that one."

Uh oh. I obviously couldn't tell the truth, and I'm a lousy liar. The commodore's face grew a darker shade of green as I scrambled for an answer.

Casey came to the rescue. "We're working on it. The flow regulator's jammed." Then she added, with a bit of edge, "From when you shot us."

The commodore remained silent for a moment. Then he forced up the corners of his mouth into what he probably considered to be a smile, and said, "Ah, the flow regulator. *Do* be careful with that. I am told they can be a little tricky. You don't want your reactor to overheat. On the other hand," the smile vanished, "if you take too long, your ship will be shredded, one blast at a time, until the faint echo of your screams is snuffed out by the void of space. You have two minutes."

Geet spun around and shook his head.

"No!" I said. "We need more time. Three minutes."

Geet shook his head again.

"Uh, no. Five!" Lousy liar, lousy negotiator.

Lusec leaned into the camera again. "Two. Minutes." Then his image disappeared, replaced on Geet's monitor by the windows that had been there earlier.

Casey leaned over and turned off the microphone. "I checked out the weapons. Two blasters at the front, one on the back. Not much compared to the Deathfighter."

Geet had somehow found a way to work even faster. "That will be enough."

Now that he had his computer back, I slipped the tablet off his lap. "We need to finish these."

Geet's eyes stayed glued to his screen. "Casey, do you know how to create a plasma surge?"

"They'll think we're actually trying to fix the engines." She set to work, fingers flying across the touchscreen keyboard. "Brilliant!"

I reopened the Gamnilians' list of demands. "Didn't Lusec say something about overheating our reactor?"

"Uh . . ." Files danced around on her screen, changing places as she inspected one, then summoned another. "That's only if you seize the flow regulator."

"So this won't do that?"

She laughed. "No! It'll blast right through it."

"But the reactor won't blow?"

"Nope." Two readouts stood side by side on her display, and her gaze flipped from one to the other. "Engines might."

"What?"

She flipped two toggle switches, then tapped a button on the computer. "There." A gentle whooshing sound arose behind us.

"Are you nuts?"

"As long as we shut it down after about 30 seconds, we should be fine."

Should be. "Okay, but we still have to get the rest of this done." I hadn't been tracking the time. "Can we even make it?"

Casey shrugged. "Geet. You just about done?"

He just shook his head.

"What's next on the list?" Casey asked as the engines' gentle hum morphed into a low, pulsating rumble.

I glanced nervously over my shoulder at the charred panel at the back of the cabin. "Uh . . . 'Transfer control of all—'"

The ship vibrated as the engines began to sound like my grandpa's old diesel truck.

"Warning: Propulsion system overload. Plasma levels at 102% capacity. Emergen—"

"Computer mute." Casey pulled up a *Propulsion Systems* readout. All four levels were in the red *Danger* zone. "What the . . . ?" She began to type furiously on the touchscreen keypad.

"What?" The shuttle shook now, and I had to raise my voice over the rumbling.

"This shouldn't be happening!"

"Can you stop it?" I asked.

"Trying!"

A banner began to scroll across the top of her screen. Large, red letters: WARNING: BACKUP REACTOR TEMPERATURE REACHING CRITICAL LEVELS.

Casey stared at the monitor. "*Backup* reactor?"

"Right!" I said. "Remember the Gamnilian ripped out a piece of the main one?" We were both yelling now.

"The backup must be smaller. That's why it's overloading. Gotta shut it down."

"No!" Geet tried to shout, but I could still barely hear him over the roaring engines. "We will need it."

"But . . ." I looked at the banner: 30 SECONDS UNTIL REACTOR BREACH.

"I am almost finished. Casey, get ready. When I tell you, use the thrusters to spin the ship around. And have the blasters ready."

Casey's thumb hovered over the red button on the joystick.

The commodore's face reappeared. "Time is up, my little friends."

Geet and Casey both dismissed the image and continued their work. It was up to me to stall him. I pushed the flashing green switch. "We need more time!"

"I *gave* you more time."

"It's our reactor. The flow regulator's seized. We're gonna blow!"

No response. I had him, for now.

A countdown replaced the banner: 10 . . . 9 . . . 8 . . .

I turned off the microphone. "Guys . . ."

Geet pressed a button. "Now!"

I grabbed the headrests for balance as the *Valiant* spun. The hulking dark mass of the Deathfighter filled our window.

"Go to *Surge*," Geet said. "A short burst."

The engines exploded to life and we shot forward.

"Blasters!" Geet cried.

Fiery orange streaks leapt ahead of us, erupting into multicoloured explosions as they slammed one after another into the shields of the Deathfighter. We were seconds away from impact.

"Aaaaaaah!" Casey bawled, thumb hard on the blasters.

Then she was gone.

32 Boom.

I dropped to the floor in darkness. Looked up. The only light came from the blurry glow of computer screens.

Someone grunted beside me. I peered through the gloom. Casey had just landed on her butt. She pushed herself up onto her haunches. "Huh?" She squinted at me, then past me. "Huh?" she repeated.

I spun to see Geet hop to his feet, then wobble off across the room. "Lights!"

Several orangey lamps lit up. Instinctively, I covered my eyes. As soon as I raised my arm I felt it: like my body had been taken apart and reassembled by a child. "You teleported us."

"Again?" Casey groaned.

I sat and looked around a cave a little bigger than a double garage. Geet now scurried along a counter that stretched almost the length of the far wall, checking the various electronic devices that were already running, and booting up those that weren't. "Yes. I am sorry," he replied, settling in at a keyboard near the middle of the counter. "This is my home. We must hurry. They will find us soon."

His fingers slid across a track pad, and an image popped up on a huge viewscreen mounted high on the cave wall above us: the Deathfighter, hanging there like a huge grey-brown storm cloud. He zoomed in for a close up until the rough, battle-scarred hull was all we could see.

Casey had stumbled ahead. Halfway across the cave she stopped and pointed up at the screen. Little bits of something floated between the camera and the massive ship. "Hey. What's that? It looks like . . ."

A headrest floated by. I swallowed hard. "The *Valiant*."

"Wow." She said it softly. Then she stepped forward and joined Geet at the computer.

The image on the viewscreen flickered, then changed: Commodore Lusec, from his folded arms up, standing in what looked like the Deathfighter's control room. "I suppose you are all feeling very clever, with your little tricks. But here are the facts: You are hiding in a hole in a rock, and there is nowhere left for you to run. Sitting on your doorstep is the flagship of the Gamnilian Empire, with the largest arsenal in the sector. You have backed yourselves into a corner. Your choices are simple: Power down your foolish toys immediately and proceed to the exit, where one of our shuttles will be arriving shortly to collect you. Or," he repositioned his arms onto his hips and leaned forward for emphasis, "wait there while we begin firing at your little pebble until it collapses around you, crushing you like—"

The outside view of the Deathfighter reappeared.

Geet set a remote control on the counter. Apparently he'd had enough of the commodore.

He turned and spoke to Casey as though nothing had happened. "I have a machine that will stop them. If you get that tablet," he pointed to a device just beyond her reach, "I will show you what to do."

As soon as she laid her hand on it, a muffled explosion shook the cave. I set my hand on the cool rock of the cave floor in order to push myself to my feet, and felt the vibrations as we were hit again.

"Activate shields," Geet called out. "Status on monitor three." There was another blast as he turned to look for me. "Simon, over there." He pointed to a computer at the far end of the counter, in a dark corner. "Watch the shields."

Once again: cool job for Casey, lame one for Simon. I made my way across the cave, stopping twice to catch my balance as Gamnilian blasters thumped into us. "They're getting closer!"

When I arrived, the screen showed a three-dimensional outline of the asteroid, slowly spinning. Our cave was roughly in the middle. Yellow and orange dots showed that the impacts were all around us and, as I'd guessed, working their way in. On the right side of the display was a bar graph labelled *Shield Strength*. The bar flashed orange. "Whoa." I called over to Geet, "Hey, we're down to 30% already!"

Geet and Casey were huddled together over her tablet. He looked up, turned to his computer and made a few quick adjustments. "How about now?" he said, just as we were hit again.

Dust drifted down onto my monitor. "Twenty-two."

"That is all I can do."

"Any weapons?" Casey asked.

"Just"—he gripped the edge of the counter as a huge explosion rocked us—"my machine. We must hurry." He went back to giving Casey directions.

The computer showed that our shields had protected us from a direct hit on our cave. For now. "Seven percent." I turned and looked along the counter. "What am I supposed to do when the shields run out?"

"Just—"

Another concussion cut him short. The little orange bar disappeared. "Gone," I said. "And they know where we are. The next hit could wipe us out!"

"They will not do that. They need you alive."

"Just him?" Casey asked.

He didn't answer. "And they want my technology. They will not destroy the cave."

Two shots hit us one after another. This time, without the shields, the vibrations shook me right down to my bones. "How long 'til your machine is ready?"

"I do not know. Soon, I hope. We must hurry."

We—meaning *Geet and Casey*—*must hurry*—meaning *shut up and let me work.* My job was just to stand and watch the Gamnilians pound away at us. Which they did again. And again.

High on the wall above Geet and Casey, the viewscreen showed the Deathfighter spitting out its fiery weapons. Three openings ran along the top of the ship, with another two on the bottom corners. An eruption would burst out from one of them, and I'd watch it fly toward us, bracing for an impact that seemed to take forever. And there was nothing I could do. Every blow that shook our little refuge felt like a punch in the face.

One seemed to soar right for the viewscreen. The whole room shook as a spray of dust and pebbles flew up in front of the camera. My gaze followed one chunk of rock as it sailed away, tumbling end over end. Just like my little meteoroid. Floating through space alone. Ripped from its home. *Children should not be taken from their families.*

I looked down at my hands, clenched into fists at my side. I lifted one and studied its shape: the thumb knuckle sticking out a little at one end, the fingers forming a lumpy ridge along the top. The meteoroid popped into my mind, and a plan began to take shape along with it.

Two more hits rocked the cave and I stumbled. Leaning forward, I placed my hands wide apart on the counter for balance, then went into my imagination. *You can do this.* The meteoroid reappeared in my mind, gently rotating, like the asteroid on the computer. Blocking out the explosions that continued around me, I saw the grey stone, its rough surface, the countless holes like little craters.

Another blast shook me, and I opened my eyes to flickering lights. "They are targeting our power," I heard Geet say.

Focus, Simon.

I dove back in. Pictured the meteoroid again, remembering every little detail. This time it took shape quickly. Around the coarse rock I saw the black emptiness of space, feeling its coldness. Finally, I recalled the view from the *Valiant's* window and one by one, distant, twinkling stars appeared in the background.

"Go!" I shouted and it launched. Picking up speed, it whizzed through clouds of pebbles and dust kicked up by the Deathfighter's assaults, faster still past the remains of the *Valiant.* Then it was a blur streaking streaking toward one of the Deathfighter's blaster ports, arriving just as a shot burst out, erupting in a white-hot explosion as the two collided.

My eyes popped open and I staggered back. Looking around, I found Casey regarding me with a mixture of confusion and concern. I gave my head a gentle shake to clear it. "A meteoroid," I said. Her gaze followed mine as I looked up at the viewscreen.

Geet, whose eyes were already on the image of the Deathfighter, called out, "Viewscreen, maximum magnification, quadrant two." The camera zoomed in on the top right blaster port, the area around it charred.

"I . . . imagined it."

"Whoa," Casey said.

Geet looked at me, brows knit. He hesitated for a moment, then asked, "Can you do it again? If they—" another shot erupted from the scarred hole, "knock out our power, we cannot use my machine." He stumbled as the weapon made contact. "If you hit a blaster port right after it fires, you can get through the shields."

I didn't know what his machine did, but I knew that if it didn't work, we were going back to the Deathfighter. Stepping up to the counter, I propped myself up on one elbow, then the other. I raised a hand and made a fist; looked at the hand lying on the counter. Clenched it. Why not? *Twins.*

I closed my eyes. Took a breath. Then, using my imagination like a sculptor's hands, I began building two meteoroids, side by side. First the basic shapes: Two potato-shaped lumps of stone appeared. Then the details: an indent here, a hard edge there, everywhere pockmarks. Much faster this time. *Easy.*

More blasts. I felt the cave shake around me, the pounding against my eardrums. But I was in the zone. Rather than simply blocking it out, I used it, sucking the power from every impact—all the noise and destruction—and feeding it into the two chunks of grey rock until I could barely hold them back.

I pictured the Deathfighter hanging in space before us. First one, then the other leapt toward it. I watched, eyes darting between them, *willing* them to their targets, following them as they streaked through the blackness. In my mind, I zoomed in on the charred port, watched the orange flash burst out, then guided the first one right into the empty hole where it exploded in a shower of rock, fire and twisted metal. Repeated it with the other, which ripped apart a second opening.

I dropped to one knee, head spinning.

Casey's face swung in my direction. "Simon! Are you—"

A warning siren sounded. My station. I reached for the counter and pulled myself to my feet. "I'm okay." But I had to lean on the counter and close my eyes for a moment to let a wave of wooziness pass.

A look at the monitor told me we'd been hit more than I'd realized. The dots had become red blotches. But that wasn't the worst news. "They blew off the bottom of the asteroid."

"They've found the generator," Geet called back.

"We can't take many more hits." I knew what I needed to do. I took a breath. Closed my eyes. *Focus, Simon.*

When the next blast smacked us, my mind followed the vibration out to the surface of the asteroid. We'd been struck dozens of times—how many bits of rock had the Gamnilian weapons torn from the surface? I pictured a hundred fragments floating in space. Zooming in on one the size of my head, I examined its surface and suddenly *knew* that even as I imagined it, it had appeared, grey and hard and jagged, above us.

I popped out of my mind and looked up at the viewscreen for just long enough to burn the image of the Deathfighter into my memory. Then I went back into my imagination, where the meteoroid awaited me. Propelling it toward the giant ship, I watched it tumble off, gaining speed, soaring, then streaking toward its mark, striking the edge of a blaster port just after a shot flew out, tearing through metal and leaving a hole big enough to fly a shuttle though.

Three ports down, two to go. Back to the floating rocks. Picked one, saw it, felt it become real. Flung it. Watched it fly even as I started the next one. Images and sounds flipped effortlessly through my mind now: Meteoroid after meteoroid appeared, shot through the sky, then exploded against the Deathfighter. Faster, until everything became a blur of light and sound and rage, racing out of control.

Then, from somewhere far beyond it all, a familiar voice, calling my name.

I let go, and it all evaporated. Listened for the voice. Let it pull me back.

"Simon!" I opened my eyes. Turned. Found Casey, near the back of the cave.

I swayed, gripped the counter.

"You got' em," she said. "You can stop."

I listened. No more explosions. "What're you doing?"

"Gamnilians are in the asteroid," she said, breathless. "I've gotta teleport 'em out. You go help Geet!"

I squinted in his direction. Raised a foot, wobbled, tipped back and slid down the stone wall, landing with a plop on the cold floor.

Darkness. Voices.

Casey. "I don't know what I'm doing over here, Geet."

"You have the coordinates," I heard him answer. "Target, lock, send. You can do it."

Fighting through the fog, I forced myself to open my eyes. Searing pain shot through my skull. I blacked out again.

"Hurry!" It was Geet.

I opened my eyes. Took a breath, then focused.

Casey adjusted a dial. "Just one left." She pressed a button.

A Gamnilian soldier appeared right in the middle of the cave.

"Uh oh." Casey adjusted the dial, but nothing happened.

I stared up at the back of the Gamnilian's bald, green head. He teetered, took a step to regain his balance. Looked around. Saw Casey, fumbling with the controls.

As I leaned forward, my hand brushed against a rock on the floor. A mini-meteoroid.

The soldier raised his gun unsteadily.

My hand swallowed up the stone as I willed myself up onto one knee. Hurled it. Watched it streak to its target. Heard it crack against his skull, throwing his rifle blast off target, sending it slamming into the cave wall far from my sister. Saw a dot of purple blood as he dropped, then disappeared before hitting the floor.

"Yes!" Casey shouted.

I slumped to the ground.

"Simon!" I heard Casey's footfalls as she raced to my side, and felt her hands gripping my shoulders. "It's okay. I got you."

"I'm fine." She helped me prop myself up on one elbow. "I just—"

There was an enormous sucking sound, the lights dimmed and the entire cave shifted.

We looked at Geet.

He said simply, "Boom."

We looked up at the viewscreen. No Deathfighter. Just space.

"Boom?" Casey repeated.

"Gone!"

"Wha—" She shook her head. "How?"

Geet giggled. "I . . . moved them."

"Moved them?"

"Yes. It is . . . a displacement cannon. I built it to protect this sector from the Gamnilians. It works!" He clapped his hands.

Casey laughed. "So . . . exactly how far did you move them?"

Again Geet smiled. "Very far. They will not be back for . . . a long, long time."

33 Beyond My Wildest Dreams

I stood in a lush, green valley. Above, the sun shone brightly in a clear, blue sky. On the hillsides around me, daisies and tall grass swayed in a gentle breeze. Everything was perfect.

Then an ugly giant appeared in front of me, his bald head blocking out the sun. He folded his muscular arms and looked down on me from far above. "Fee-fi-fo-fum," he bellowed.

"What?" I said. "I don't understand. Speak English."

"You're not tall!" he replied, reaching for a gun he had tucked into the waist of his pants.

I stepped toward him. Raised a fist. It turned to stone. I jumped up and punched him right in one of his beady little eyes. "Boom," I said, as he disappeared.

*   *   *

After Geet moved the Gamnilians, he and Casey had helped me to my feet. With one of them on either side of me for support, we'd made our way through a passageway that connected several smaller caves to the first. We entered a cozy one that appeared to be his living space, and he showed me to a pile of cloth and pillows off in a corner. It was his bed, he said, though it looked more like a nest. I'd fallen asleep soon after, Geet and Casey's soft conversation my lullaby.

I don't remember dreaming at first—I was out cold. But the longer I slept, the more I dreamt, and the more I dreamt, the weirder it got. After the giant disappeared, I heard movement in the grass off to one side. I turned to see a fluffy, caramel-coloured bunny, sitting up on its hind legs, nose twitching. It looked up at me with huge brown eyes. "Hello," it said in a voice that seemed very familiar. "I wanted to . . . show you . . . something." Then it raised a paw and pointed off behind me.

On a hilltop across the valley stood a huge rock formation: grey, 20 stories tall, and roughly the shape of a potato. I was sure it hadn't been there before, so I turned to ask the bunny about it. I found it clapping its paws together joyfully. When I opened my mouth to ask where the rocks came from, it said, "It is . . . complicated." Then it giggled hysterically and dove headfirst into its hole.

I looked up at the hilltop again. The stone was shimmering. As I watched, it distorted and shifted, changing before my eyes into a bunch of storage crates and barrels. The way they were stacked seemed very familiar: much lower than the rocks, more wide than tall, and sort of boxy.

Once again, whatever-it-was on the hill began to blur, the containers warping and changing colour until the whole thing morphed into something I recognized immediately: our house!

My heart leapt, and I set off toward it at a run. But only a few short strides later, another bunny popped out of another hole, stopping me in my tracks. This one was purple, and much larger than the first one—though the bottom half of him was below ground, the tips of his ears rose almost to chest height.

"Congratulations, Simon!" he said in a cheesy voice. "It's the *bonus round*!" He flashed a grin that revealed two rows of perfect, made-for-television teeth. "Are you ready?"

I looked up at my house. "Uh . . ."

"Of *course* you are!" He paused to wink at a camera that didn't exist. "Simon, for 1 billion points, how many cow turds are on Uranus?"

Enough of this. I needed to get home. I darted off to one side, but an arm shot out of his purple chest. A piece of

246

paper was stuck on the end of it, which he thrust in my face. "Don't you wanna see my report card?" he whined.

I ducked under the arm and sprinted for the hill. Looking over my shoulder, I saw Purple Bunny clutching the paper tightly, bawling. Before I had a chance to turn around, I slammed into something at full speed, knocking me onto my backside. There, one foot on either side of a rabbit hole, stood Commodore Lusec. He towered above me, wearing my mother's favourite blue dress.

"Wha . . . what . . . ?" I babbled.

He set his hands on his hips and leaned forward, his beady eyes narrowing dangerously. "Please state your request in the form of a specific question or command," he said.

I blinked. Opened my mouth. Closed it.

The commodore clicked his heels together and was sucked back down into the hole.

I rose warily to my feet. Looked up at my house. Took one step toward it.

Soft yellow light began to glow within the burrow. I stopped in time to see it shoot up, projecting a life-size hologram of Geet that hovered almost high enough off the ground to look me in the eyes. "Hello, Simon."

I waited. Any second, he'd turn into a cow, or start talking in farts.

"It is really me."

"Uh huh. And I'm the prime minister of Canada."

"Do you remember the Doctor's brain probe?" he asked. "After you and Casey fell asleep, I made a few changes to one of my machines. So I can talk to you."

It did *feel* like him. The first bunny's voice had sounded right, but I never actually thought it was *him*.

"You are still asleep." Holo-Geet stepped down onto the grass. "The machine is feeding my voice into your dream."

"Why?"

"It is time," he said softly.

"Time for what?"

"For you to . . ." He lowered his head. "Go home."

I looked up at the top of the hill.

"Your *real* home."

The house on the hill faded into nothingness.

"How?"

"The same way you got here." He turned and began walking up the slope. "By imagining."

I watched him from the bottom of the hill. "But I tried that before. On the *Valiant*."

"You were not ready then," he said without looking back. "Now you are."

But I wasn't. "This is a dream. I can't control my dreams."

"It is *your* mind." Somehow he was already standing on top of the hill. His voice was gentle and soft as always, yet I heard him clearly. "*Your* dreams, *your* memories, *your* imagination. *You* decide what to do with them."

I wasn't convinced, but I began the climb toward him.

"Why are you walking?" he asked. "Fly."

"What?"

He hopped up into the air, shot straight up several metres, then swooped down like a bird, stopping to hover just ahead of me, as if he was a hologram again. He clapped his hands and giggled. "It is fun!"

I loved flying dreams, but I could never make them happen on purpose. And when they did happen, they always ended in disappointment: I'd take off, then almost immediately start to sink back down to the ground.

In a blink Geet was at my side, reaching out to me. "Here. Together."

I took his hand.

He bent his knees and counted down. "Three, two, one. Go!" We jumped, shooting into the air almost effortlessly, soaring up and over the top of the hill. Still we rose, arms spread wide, only levelling out when the daisies were just tiny white specks far below. We sailed along like that for a while, breathlessly soaring over a blanket of green rolling hills that stretched to the horizon in every direction.

Geet let go of my hand and dropped into a dive. Far below, he banked right, darted back up, then looped back around to fall in beside me again. "Try it!"

I banked, first left, then right. No problem. So I dove down, then halfway to the grass below, swept right and shot up into a loop-the-loop. "Woohoo!"

Geet appeared beside me, giggled, then tapped me on the shoulder. "You're it!" he said, then flew off. I tore after him, and we chased each other across the brilliant blue sky until finally—after what felt like it could have been minutes, hours or days—we lowered ourselves onto the cool grass on top of the hill where we'd started.

Geet sat down, wrapping his arms around his knees. I joined him, plucking a long piece of grass, twirling it between my fingers as we sat together in silence, gazing across the valley. Several minutes passed. "Geet . . ."

He looked over at me.

"How come . . . for the last two days, all I've wanted is to go home. Now I can, and . . . I wanna stay?"

"Feelings are . . . complicated." He smiled, but his enormous brown eyes glistened, and he looked away.

"Yup." The truth was I still wanted to go home just as much as before. I just didn't want to leave Geet.

"You will be back."

"Really?"

"Yes."

"When? How?"

"I . . . do not know." He looked out across the valley again. "This is new, and we both have much to learn. But," he turned his face toward mine again, "I know *some* things. Like, you must go back home. It is where you belong. But you belong here too now—both of you do. You are connected to this universe. To me."

I knew he was right. I didn't know how. *Complicated.*

We were both quiet for a little while.

"So, what do I do?"

"Just like before. Dream. Imagine."

I nodded.

"Lie down," he said. "Relax."

I lay back in the grass, closed my eyes, took a long breath and blew it out slowly.

"Now picture home. Where were you when you left?"

The game show. "Sitting on the couch."

"Good," he said. "Start there. Imagine the room around you. The walls, the floor. Everything, just the way it was."

I began with the entertainment unit, remembering the black wood and some of the odds and ends on the shelves. I stopped when I got to the family picture that sat all by itself to one side. It was old—Casey and I were maybe five when it was taken. Dad had lost some hair since then, and Mom had gained some weight. I wondered what would happen if I imagined us all like the picture instead of the way we actually were. Mom and Dad would probably like it, but I didn't want to be five again.

I shook my head to clear it.

"Relax," Geet said, "and focus."

I looked up at the ceiling and saw the crack that had been there, like a tiny lightning bolt, for as long as I could remember. I focused on the wall, and the beige paint. Mom repainted every few years, and each time, after looking at a thousand paint swatches, it ended up being just another shade of beige. I smiled, then looked down at the hardwood floor. Little bits of the remote control were scattered across the area between the couch and the television.

I let my gaze wander to the brown fabric of the couch. It looked rough, like a meteoroid. I ran my hand across it, pressed it down, feeling it give, noticing how comfortable it felt beneath me. I lifted my feet off the floor, bent my knees, tucked my legs to one side. Then I reached for a light blue pillow, stuffed it under my arm and leaned over onto the armrest.

"Good." Geet's voice seemed to be coming from far away. "You are almost there. Now your sister."

Casey appeared almost all at once. I didn't even have to try. I just looked over at the armchair, and there she was, leaning forward, staring at the television. She blinked. "Hey!" she said, looking around. "We're—"

The sound of bells clanging pulled our attention to the TV. "You know what that means, folks." It was the same cheesy game show host we'd been watching when we left. He cranked his grin up one more notch until the whiteness of his perfect teeth hurt my eyes. "It's time for our . . . *final question!*" Cue dramatic music. "Ready, contestants? For 1,000 points: What is the greatest distance any human has ever traveled in space?"

I looked at Casey.

She looked at me.

And we both laughed our heads off.

We were home.

Acknowledgements

Big thanks to my family, of course, for supporting me in more ways than I can name. To my sons, specifically, for being this book's first audience a long time ago. And for demanding all the other bedtime stories that both made me a better storyteller, and went a long way toward making me believe I could actually write a book someday.

Feedback is invaluable to a writer, and I'm very grateful to the members of Red Deer's *Writers' Ink* for the insight and encouragement they offered. In particular, I must thank John Burnham, who is pretty much the perfect critique partner: lots of positives, and all kinds of ideas that improved the manuscript. Speaking of such things, I'm very grateful to my son Matt, who eagerly sought out each new revision (largely to avoid his own work, but still) and offered invaluable advice that vastly improved the final product. Perhaps his greatest accomplishment lay in averting the overutilization of headlamps in this novel. Sadly, however, he was unable to mitigate the incidence of storage crates and barrels. It's my book, after all. And I'm the dad.

Finally, my former students: Thanks for sharing a little bit of your childhood with me. I think it rubbed off! Many of you heard an earlier version of this story, and insisted that I get it published. I said I would, so here it is.

About the Author

Robin Pawlak was a teacher for 31 years in Red Deer, Alberta (Canada). He had boatloads of fun with his students, but three decades is a long time, so he decided to retire to something a little quieter. Nowadays, he spends most of his time in his office, making stuff up and muttering to himself. Some say this is a sure sign that all that time with children drove him mad. This may be true. But if one writes his imaginings down, he can call himself an *author*, which is a somewhat more respectable title than *lunatic*.

If you visit robinpawlak.com, you'll find even more of Robin's madness on display. You can also follow Robin on Twitter @1robinstweet, as well as on Instagram and Facebook as 1robinpawlak.

Please also consider leaving a review on Amazon. Aside from buying their books, reviews are the best way to support independent authors!

Gamnilian Translation Guide

Includes all Gamnilian lines, in order (chapters in parentheses).

Hakh'k na'tek! (11)
You not move! (Or, *Do not move!*)

Hakh'k dahg, hakh'k mikh'nahg. (11)
You try, you painfully die. (a popular Gamnilian threat)

Na'tek! (11)
Not move!

Dja'sh'k! Hakh'k na'pekh, trrikkit breex'nikh't'ahng trroolaht! (11)
&#@*#@! You keep going, pretty &@#*@# coward!
(Calling a male *pretty* is considered a huge insult, as is calling him a coward. &@#*@# isn't awesome either.)

Bekh! (11)
@&*#@#!

Hakh'k ja'kah'mikh'ja t'k? (11)
You challenge me?

T'k xahg'daht hakh'k ja'kah'mikh'ja. (11)
I give you challenge. (As in, *I'll give you a challenge!*)

Kahk'pakht. Hakh'k ch'n'kaht vik, agzsh'k't'kaw! (11)
Take over. You fix it, #&@*@#!
(*Kahk'pakht* means *to take over* or *seize victoriously*, so there is some sarcasm here, as in, *Congratulations! You have won, oh mighty one, so I surrender this to you!*)

Hakh'k m'kiti pakka'tuuk! Kiti kekh'maash! T'k— (11)
You tiny #@#*&@! Little insect! I—
(A *kekh'maash* is a despised Gamnilian insect. To call someone a *kekh'maash* is a great insult, suggesting that they are cunning, but in a cowardly way.)

J'bok! Shah'k'tang sss'k sh'bekh. (11)
Hey! Duty before pleasure.
(*Shah'k'tang sss'k sh'bekh—Duty before pleasure*—is a Gamnilian saying of military origin that is commonly used to remind others of a basic Gamnilian value. Said to a person of greater authority, it is likely to be received as an insult.)

Na'ghaht, kiti'k! D'at'na'tahk t'k hxah'k'tang, t'k tahn'nahg hakh'k sh'k ch'n'kaht vik t'k'sha! (11)
Silence, child! If I must, I kill you and fix it myself!

Pekh'vik! T'k na'krroo na'nikh'da sh'mahg'tet hakh'k sh'da— (11)
Stop it! I not need help from you for—

Hxa-a-abh! T'k kuh'k'tahg tuh'lagh! (11)
&@#@#! I rise now!
(*T'k kuh'k'tahg tuh'lagh—I rise now*—is a Gamnilian expression spoken by those about to do something great or heroic. We might say, *This is my moment.*)

Baxa! Tuh'lagh! Na'daw'tek. Ah'tekh. (11)
Get up! Now! Move quickly. Ah'tekh.
(An *ah'tekh* is a four-legged Gamnilian animal similar to a dog, but about the size of a small donkey and of low intelligence. Formerly used as beasts of burden, modern technology has made them unnecessary. Now they run wild in packs and are seen as nuisances.)

F'kiti'k. F'kiti'ka'makh. (11)
Little ones. Little appetizers.

V'tik. (11)
a call to attention, specifically used by those in authority to announce their presence and/or get the attention of their subordinates

Kiti'tek t'an! Shah akht! (11)
Shuffle back! Ready stance! *(These are both military commands.)*

Tahk'makh. (12)
Tahk'makh means *bog food*, a very common and popular dish, especially in or near the southern Boglands. It is made of roasted *djar'ba* bladder, *kha'bawk'naht* intestines heated over fire in their own (ample) juices, and the blood of *nuhrf*s. All three creatures are native to the southern Boglands.

djar'ba (12)
a fat, short-legged greyish-purple creature that is otherwise similar to a pig or boar and which lives in hot, humid climates near bogs or marshes

kha'bawk'naht (12)
a bog-dwelling creature with some of the characteristics of snakes, lizards and alligators. They can be up to 4 metres long and 1.5 metres wide at their midpoint (stomach and intestines), though most of their body is narrower.

J'bok! (12)
Hey!

Tuhg? (12)
What?

Gikh. (12)
Bread.

Bahn'akh'tee? (12)
Why?

F'dawkh'k'tang. Khit'k meel makh mahg'tet khit'k. (12)
Orders. They want food to them.

Pikh f'jahg. (15)
Two chairs.

**Chahkh'b'xahg'daht'nahg! Nee'xahg'daht
kiti'hakh'k'sha tuh'lagh'na'daw.** (25)
Pilot! Tell identity immediately.

bahkh (29)
a small, almost hairless creature similar in size and body
shape to a ferret, but without a tail. They are scavengers,
often stealing their food from other creatures, including
Gamnilians.

Pahkht! (29)
Pow! *(imitating the sound of a blaster)*

T'k dja'tang. K'dekh. (29)
I obey. End.

**Ba'neel't'nek d'at'na'tahk mot'k dawkh'k'tang f't'k
mahg'tet tahn'nahg mot'k.** (31)
Only if he order us to kill him.

*This translation guide along with a Gamnilian dictionary
(and other cool stuff!) can be found at robinpawlak.com.*

Made in the USA
Columbia, SC
01 April 2018